Power Riches Or Death -PROD
Vol. I
THE KINGMAKER

POWER RICHES OR DEATH - PROD VOL. 1

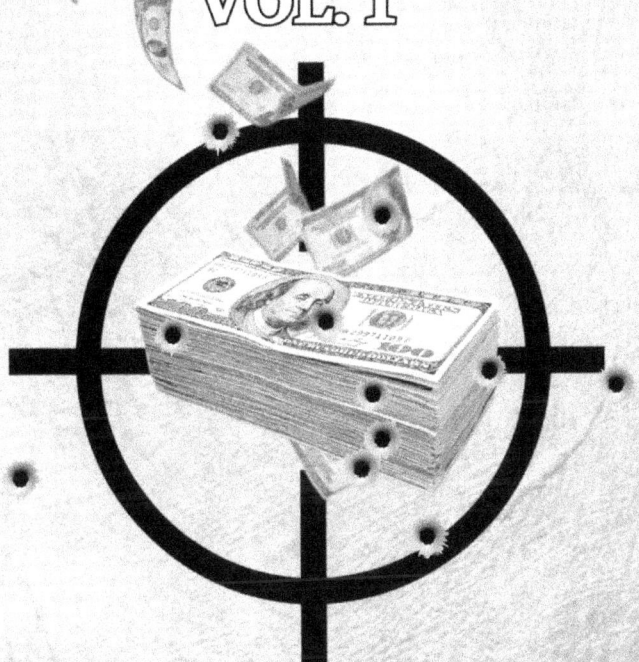

THE
KINGMAKER

CHARLES FLAGG

Power Riches Or Death- PROD Vol. I, THE KINGMAKER
© 2025, by Charles Flagg

ISBN: 979-8-9879871-6-2

Published by: Regal Rhythms Poetry LLC
Printed in the United States of America

Edited by: Regal Rhythms Poetry LLC
Cover Art : Adam Hayden

ACKNOWLEDGEMENTS

I thank everyone who supported me throughout this life changing dream making process.

CONTENTS

Chapter 1

Heart, water, and smiley face emojis from an unsaved number was the good morning and thank you text, as my phone vibrated on my night stand, it woke me from a deep much needed sleep. My cooking class went very well last night, a longtime patron of my show suggested that I invite her over to work on some recipes together. No inhibitions, just manifestation. The deep tissue massages combined with sensual instrumentals allowed her mystique to escape from under her mask, even if it was only for the night. The conservative exterior was armor that she used to repress her sexuality. Liberation was what her soul cried out to me. A liberator was what I was.

An executive that wore business attire and gave orders all throughout her day, and appreciated relieving stress from the demands of her daily life. Her nature surrendered in full submission to my masculine presence.

A confident woman who wasn't comfortable showing her vulnerability, unless it's away from prying and judgmental eyes.

"You can be your complete self with me. Here, there are no masks or costumes," I convinced.

Feeling reassured, she agreed with subtle gestures using only her eyes. Her shoulders began to relax, slowly shedding her armor layer by layer. Confidence increased as each layer hit the floor. Skin tone like a bronze Madonna statue was shining from her moisturizer. She tensed up momentarily not wanting to reveal the scar on her left thigh, her eyes told the story while looking down and away from me.

Methodically, I began rubbing her thigh, slowly bringing her attention back to me, she spoke in a guarded demure tone, "I don't know why I'm so insecure about this scar."

"We can discuss that later," I said, extending my hand. She took a few steps towards me, her hands soft, but full of strength. A foot or so shorter than I am, it felt like I was towering over her. I stared into her unique greenish brown eyes, detecting her true desires, intensely simmering ready to erupt. With a handful of her hair, I engaged those flames, and dared them to engulf me. Her lips were soft and sweet like a ripe melon. "I'm so wet. It's been awhile," she confessed unsolicited, rubbing herself just below the naval as she spoke. Nothing else for me to confess, I hoisted her up like a trophy. Placed myself inside her secret garden inch by inch, worked my way to her very origin. She latched her thick thighs around me while I maneuvered myself deeper inside of her.

She bellowed in a sultry tone, "I need to be fucked! Pound all of this stress out of me, please!"

Words spoken from her soul. She said exactly what she wanted to say. I said nothing. I just pounded that pussy up against the wall. Massaged her inside out, making it messy just the way she wanted it. Slightly off and out of rhythm, cause' she was anxious, but then we began to flow. Sweat beaded and dripped from her skin.

Our bodies collided forging something unknown, but beautiful. She straddled me, thrusting from her core, while my left hand gripped her throat firmly. My right thumb inside her mouth, she sucked and teased it with her tongue. Her body began to rattle, thrusting harder and faster on my curved erection. "Yes, that's my spot," she whispered in between moans exploding all over my chiseled mid-section. Her eyes rolled in the back of her head, biting my thumb in the process. The adrenaline did not allow me to feel the pain. Too deep into the moment to pause. Slow, deep, and repeatedly, I continued getting everything out that she was

3

holding back. Her body flimsy and her legs numb, I stood up, cradling her, and dug deep inside of her under the moonlight. She was open, so I couldn't help but go the extra mile.

"Oooh damn, I can feel you in my stomach. You going' deep deep," she moaned.

"I'm finna' go deeper than this," I vocalized with pleasure.

My inner savage had awakened, so the inner savage was what I gave her. The moans increased intensifying my hardness. Feeling myself swell, I slowed my strokes and controlled my breathing, cause' I didn't want to cum yet. I bent her over the edge of the terrace and stirred her slow and deep some more.

"Oh my God, look what you're doing to me, I'm so wet," she delighted. Her inner thighs were drenched as I stretched and molded her tight wet pussy. Her walls giving way every time I rubbed against her ridges.

"You can cum again. I want you to cream all over this dick," I told her while nibbling on her earlobe. I looked down at the glossy shine on my erection in-between strokes.

"I'm gonna try! I came too many times! I can't feel my legs," the words poured from her mouth with satisfication and exhaustion. I growled as I came all over her butterfly tattoos on her spine.

After dessert we enjoyed the entrée: seared prime fillets cooked to a juicy medium, charred brussel sprouts with Chipotle honey glaze and grilled asparagus with lemon garlic butter. We fed each other with our hands straight from the pots and pans while standing nude in front of the stove. It felt barbaric, but right. The food was just fuel for the next round. We both knew that.

Chapter 2

Gazing at the clear blue sky almost hypnotically, I enjoyed the breeze, and the panoramic view from the comfort of my bedroom. Being from the city, I ain't use' to this extremely warm weather this time of year. When I journeyed down here many years ago, I was a heavy drinking, unemployed, divorcee who didn't have any idea of what type of life I wanted. My brother gave me a place to stay; from there, I came up with a game plan to stand firmly back on my feet. A hot cup of green tea with a drop of raw honey always gets my juices flowing after my morning run and workout. I can't remember who suggested adding a pinch of cinnamon, I still hadn't gotten around to it yet.

Dr. Sarita Monday, who I affectionately called Stormy, introduced me to this healthier lifestyle a few months ago. We met at a concert at the Staples Center about five years or so ago. It wasn't love at first sight, but it was as if I had sight for the first time. For others, she would appear out of their league; however, she was the perfect league for me.

Wrapped in a custom white dress blanketed with stargazing lilies that caressed every curve and contour of her soft fit body. She smelled like fresh rosewater and honey dews. Handcrafted fire red locs flowed then rested in the middle of her back. Fingernails long enough to scratch my itch and short enough to handle business. Her matching toenails were on display through her open toe heels. We were walking in opposite directions; the mutual attraction was instant and obvious. I complimented on her diamond and amethyst hourglass medallion, that became the segway to our introduction. We spent time walking and talking throughout the venue, never returning to our seats. After we exchanged contact information, we never stopped speaking or seeing one another except for our spats and momentary break ups.

My time travel was interrupted by my cellphone as a Facebook picture of Isis Grey flashed and vibrated. I stared back at the Avatar debating whether to answer it or not. Isis is a very talented multi-medium artist that has been constantly rising from the local ranks to international acclaim. I have an Atlas sculpture that she created for me just to show her appreciation for an on-air interview, but her begging ass gets on my nerves.

"Isis, what's up. You know I don't like calls this early unless it's about business," I barked.

In typical Isis fashion, she ignored my words and proceeded to speak, "Craft, I know it seems like I always want something when I call, but this time, I want to give you something."

"I don't look at you in that way, "Pancake," but thanks for the offer."

"You are such a Pig! … I want you to model for this adult erotic paint and sip show that I will be teaching and hosting," said the former starving artist with the flap jack booty.

She has some of the prettiest brown almond-colored eyes I have seen since Shannon (what's her name) back in elementary school.

"It's definitely exposure for your upcoming book "Pages of Sad Poems," and not to mention your podcast," Isis continued without ceasing, bribing me, and trying to gas me with flattery.

"You've been working out. Showoff that chiseled body that's inspiration to women everywhere that their Boaz does exist," Isis lectured.

"Flattery will get you nowhere," I reminded her.

"What do you mean, so do we have a deal or not?" she badgered.

"Let me think about it Isis. As long as it doesn't conflict with any previous engagements, I'm up to the challenge," I responded, trying to get her off the phone.

"I heard getting it up is never a challenge. When are you going to invite me over for a morning run or cooking class?" she proposed.

"Run the particulars by Dick Brownstein, and he will get back to you as soon as we have the final numbers. Isis, you know I'm about my paper," I said, ending the call abruptly .

Isis threw my rhythm off for a lil'minute, but on a positive note, it was an opportunity to expand my brand as well as recruit new clients. More business cards printed, and T-Shirts need to be made especially for this event. If it's money to get, I got something to flip. Walked in my bathroom that is three times as big as the bedroom I had down in the basement of my brother's house when I first arrived here. Being in that basement allowed me to stare at myself beyond the reflection in the mirror. I saw myself manifested through the storm and aligned with the universe. Once my distractions were eliminated, I minimized my habits and maximized my hustle. Now, I'm enjoying the fruits of my labor. One of the greatest decisions I could have made.

Chapter 3

Surround sound delivered music in HD, when I showered or soaked in the tub, depending on the day. Large infinity windows allowed the natural sun light to illuminate my mornings. All these hi-tech amenities were installed by Rico "Turtle Tail" Glades and his wife which are both fantastic at what they do. The heated floor was my favorite.

Growing up, we would use old towels to step onto the floor from the shower. When the electricity was off in the winter, them' damn towels did little good. The scar on my left thumb was from a candle that burned too low. It was carried by an anxious child moving too fast. That was a humble reminder of the moments when a candlelight was the only light we had. There are a myriad of reminders and mementos that keep me grounded. Even though a rose can grow from the concrete, it is still best to plant seeds in fertile soil.

My clothes were organized, nearly OCD'ish, some still with the tags on them. One section business, the other section pleasure. Clothes displayed in harmonic ascending hues from lightest to darkest; denim to linen; and baseball caps to fedoras. Nevertheless, I threw on my favorite pair of heavily worn blue jeans and a green ROMAN C1RCUS T-shirt by Titan Exclusives, one of my first companies that I created. I finished off the look with some custom footwear by a mentee of one of my homeboys from the after school program down at the REC.

Richard Brownstein, who prefers everyone to call him Dick, is a middle-aged, short, Jewish guy who looks like Danny DeVito in that old Batman movie. He stands about a foot and a half taller, but still just as round.

"Brownstein," I commanded the automatic dial feature in my car. "Dick, how is it going?"speaking in the air as the call connected. The former public defender turned business-man was someone I got linked up with through Mr. Hustler International himself, my nigga, Paper Tags.

"Same o'l, same o'l, Craft. How close are you to completing that final draft? I got Shona Evans from marketing breathing down my neck about deadlines. That's what happens when you mix business with pleasure. You can't say I never told you so," Dick tried to correct me.

"Hold on! Look Dick. I didn't call to get a lecture from you. Get your damn panties out of a bunch. The deadline isn't for another two weeks, so don't worry. Did Isis give you a call about me modeling at that adult workshop for her?" I inquired.

"I haven't been into the office yet. I have to check my messages," Dick said, running late as usual.

"When you do speak with her, get the particulars on merchandising and alcohol sales, how many she expects to attend, and her marketing budget. Get back to me as soon as everything is in writing and ready to move forward."

"Anything else your majesty?" replied the twice divorced manager and cheap cigar smoker.

"That's all for now Dick," I ended the call.

Onward to the barbershop, so I can get super fresh for the festivities. Posted at the exit ramp was a man with a long, smoke-stained beard and glassy, bloodshot, red eyes. He sat on an old milk crate and scribbled his demands on a piece of cardboard, meeting his deadline. He was getting his story ready for the day. My first time being off in a while, I didn't have work on my mind. A whole week of leisure and pleasure, then back to the heavy grind of running a conglomerate.

Ira was on his way back into the freshly remodeled store front, with the broom in his hand, after sweeping up. He had been home from the pen for a few years now. The eclectic, spiritualist, and griot carried the same muscular build that those five years away sculpted with the scars from a crime unspecified. Standing like a giant Sequoia with a bark as dark as lacquer, that nearly hid his tattoos of Malcolm and Martin that were boldly inked on his massive forearms. You can spot the ancient alchemist from a mile away with the golden ankh medallion and Egyptian hieroglyphs carved into it.

I parked in my reserved spot and crossed the threshold ten minutes late to my appointment with my sexy vibrant barber for over four years. "Ice," because she was cold under pressure during her collegiate volleyball days up north at Michigan. An ACL or MCL injury ended her career during the last game of her senior year. I towered over her maybe four to five inches depending on the shoes she has on. Very well put together, even if she was running to the grocery store, no pajamas, or bonnet. She kept it simple and sexy.

"J. Craft, you're late again for the third time in as many weeks!" was her introduction in a tone I'm all too familiar with.

"My bad, "Bae", a business call took a little longer than expected. How is your day going so far beautiful?" I said, possibly pandering.

After embracing a few hands of the regulars in the shop, I gently kissed Ice on the cheek before taking my seat in the chair in front of her.

"Don't be trying to get fresh with me. I heard you been messing around with boujee, Shona Evans," Ice said with sass.

"Somebody lying on me baby. You know you're the only one for me," I replied jokingly.

"I can always tell when you're lying. That's why I won't give you the time of day," she complained, rolling her eyes with her lips twisted.

"No matter how hard I try, you will never allow me to taste your poetry, huh?"

"I'm a full feature film. You just stick to those lil' Haikus you're used to," Ice laughed and dapped Ira, or "Big I" as we call him. He was her barber in crime at the station next to us.

"Oh, so now I'm the topic of barbershop gossip?" I turned my head to address my accusers.

"I am not the one to be vested into anyone's personal affairs my brother," said the slow talking tree of a man with the keloid ear. "Besides, who you decide to lay with is your business. Just be wise brother, energies, and diseases travel on certain frequencies," Big I preached.

"Here you go, "Big I" with that mysticism shit again," I said kinda salty .

"Gimme the usual beautiful," I said, speaking directly to my barber.
She leaned the chair back with the attitude that I love to incite. Placed the steaming hot towel securely around my face, she continued, "That's your problem you never want to listen to nobody."

I was on my way to sleep, finally feeling relaxed. My eyes were closing, as my pores opened, thinking about the dream I had a few nights back. I was freefalling backwards from the terrace of my penthouse into a deep abyss of darkness, wearing only an off-white bed sheet screaming and attempting to break my fall.

There was nothing to grab a hold of, but I held on to the ominous words spoken by my grandmother, "Jont'e, you're blessed beyond measure, sent with the purpose to go beyond yourself. Why do you choose to live contrary to whom you are and who you are meant to be?" My grandmother wouldn't word it in that way, but it was her voice that is something I won't ever forget. I still call to listen to old messages just to hear her voice.

Chapter 4

Ice got me together as usual. I noticed the bags under my eyes in the mirror. I gave her the money in my left pocket, so she could take care of what's needed at the shop.

"Craft, I need to speak with you for a moment", Ice whispered in my ear to follow her outside.

"Hey Peewee, go ahead and get in the chair. I will be back in a few minutes,"she said to the old face, short stature regular. I was outside waiting looking at my cellphone while she arranged her next appointment.

"What was' you and Ira discussing? You got me waiting all long when you know I got things to do," I expressed, feeling anxious.

"You always cranky when you wake up. I'm worried about you. You've been talking in your sleep the past few appointments and I'm just worried you're working too much- " she articulated with concern.

"Ain't no need to worry, me hustling like this got the shop renovated. You know that other stuff we talked about. I'm just waiting on you to finally be ready to make that jump," I interrupted.

18

"I will talk to you about that later. I'm concerned about your health. You are talking about things that can be replaced," she declared.

"Ice, I gotta go baby. Is everything fine with you and the shop?"

"Yeah, everything is fine. Is everything good with you, is the question?" she contended.

"I'm good. I have a few deadlines to meet, but that's what I hustle for to be busy and making the moves that count," I reminded her.

"Could you look away from the phone and look at me?" she requested.

"Hey babe, this is Church calling. I gotta go. I will call you later."

"I know you won't," she spoke in a distressed tone.

"We gonna have to agree to disagree," I motioned with my hands. I hopped in my drop, pulled off from the curb. She's probably right, thinking to myself.

Back at the house, I laid on the couch and drank some herb tea with CBD, and washed down my leftover fried chicken wings from Big Barbs. All these channels and it ain't never nothing on T.V. The thought crossed my mind that my grandma is in heaven thinking I'm living so cursed in my semi-sedated state. The remote fell in the back of the couch between the pillows and interrupted my cat nap. In the process, I retrieved a pair of obsidian black panties Shona left. They were soft and sensual to the touch. I placed them under my nose and smelled the light scent of lavender that remained. With her, there was no need to ask. She knew what to do and how to do it.

Her voice saying, "Pleasing you, pleases me!" is exactly what I wanted to hear. Yeah, I know it's script, but I enjoyed how we acted it out.

That night she came over. It was raining real heavy. Thunder rattled the windows and lightening split the sky open. All she wore was a black cashmere and mink overcoat with a matching panty set from one of those exclusive boutiques she's an ambassador for. Her skin is the color of a golden peach cobbler just blowing in the wind as it cooled on the window seal early in the morning. Black six inch stilettoes with gold plated spikes conveniently were placed at the toe and heel of her shoes.

We first met at an invitation only soiree. We were transported by sprinter vans and blindfolded to an underground entrance with no address. It was just a path illuminated by torches shaped like zodiac signs. She wore a red dress that fit her body like a layer of skin, beautiful soft backside, and nice natural perky breast. A straight-laced black wig flowed with the shape of her face. A red and gold mask covered everything but her full sexy lips. The eyes that peered through the slits knew no innocence just as mine knew no guilt. Articulate and intelligent with a high sex IQ, I was drawn in like a moth to a burning flame.

In the other rooms, there were many of the finest and highest paid public servants and elected officials. They were also electing to serve up their privates away from the eyes of the public. These same people are considered role models, so their freak flag can only fly amongst the private and select.

Taking her soft well-manicured hand, I lead her to the gazebo with the 20-foot waterfalls surrounded by Magnolia trees. Whispered poetry in her ear, I slowly kissed her on the back of her neck. With every word, her skin smelled like a tropical summer. Her form-fitting dress was candy coating to her forbidden fruit. Flawless and well-tailored, not a blemish to be revealed. Her raw femininity brazenly commanded the heavens above to take notice.

Lifting her dress up slowly, I spread her legs while massaging her pussy from behind. Gently, I rubbed her juicy fruit in a slow circular motion with the first two fingers on my right hand, and a nice firm grip of her neck with my left. Her nipples swelled as her body became warmer to my touch. Her moans that she could no longer hold back, replaced the sound of the water crashing on the rocks flowing through the stream. She was my drum and I her drummer as we played a tandem improvising on percussion.

She laid on the bar under the moonlight like a sacrifice on the alter. Her chocolate covered strawberry was so sweet. With every touch, it rained sugar water. Unable to resist, I licked my finger to sample her nectar and awakened my bulging manhood like a sleeping giant. Her long legs opened wide. Her body sang an enchanted melody to me while my tongue slowly danced on her clitoris writing my name in cursive like an autograph.

My taste buds were like suction cups as I sopped her up. She moaned to the heavens every time my lips met her lips and my tongue met her clit. Her back arched as she grabbed the back of my head and pushed my face deeper inside of her. A beautiful crash that made an art out of warfare without the catastrophes, my tongue was the paintbrush swirling in an array of colors creating waves in her Lotus flower.

She begged me to insert myself inside of her while she squirmed and climaxed continuously like her favorite song on repeat. My erection was hard and mighty like Everest, but I denied myself knowing she would come in handy. Lifting her mask, I placed my fingers in her mouth. I still refused to see her face. I sought her, now she will seek me.

The tea had me zoning and feeling good. It was poker night over Turtle's house. I needed to see what he wanted me to bring. I was once a heavy drinker like my father, but a few DUI's and a divorce helped to cure me. My mother would remind me that she named the right child after him.

"I'm a work in progress," would be my only reply, followed by a kiss on her forehead.

"Hey Turtle, what's popular?" was my introduction to my monotone, hen-pecked, castle building friend.

"Today is a great day. Everything is on me tonight. Just bring your cash and your appetite," he boasted. I paused briefly to look at the phone. This cheap nigga never treated to anything.

"Did you hit the lottery, big money? We both know your cheap ass don't never spend no bread,"I said in curiosity.

"Naw, just blessed. Me and Martha signed a contract to renovate multiple commercial complexes the other day, so tonight we're celebrating amongst our closest friends and family," he boasted, attempting to be humble.

"Congratulations! Turtle, to the both of you."

He threw me off for a second, cause' I was supposed to be a part of a similar deal. We will discuss that later. I wanted to look him square in the eyes to recognize if it's bullshit or not.

Testing the waters, I said, "On another note, Church is in town. I'm bringing him through with me."

"I don't mind if Church comes. He just better know how to hold his liquor, cause' ain't no more ass whoopin passes left," Turtle threatened.

Turtle was an ex-boxer turned contractor when his boxing career didn't take off. Trying to keep up with the whereabouts of Martha kept him from keeping up with the whereabouts of the title.

I attempted to plead,"When are you and Church going to bury the hatchet?"

"That hatchet been buried. This is a time for celebration. Everything is good over this way and if it ain't good with him, he can stay over that way." I ended the call knowing this might get ugly if Church is in rare form tonight. Niggas letting women get in between them again.

Chapter 5

The shower hot and steamy, this was exactly what was needed to work some of this tension out of my muscles. The Diamond King played through the speakers getting me hyped and ready for the turn up. It's been awhile since I kicked it with my homeboys. This was the perfect time for Church to come through and bend a few corners. I know Church was going to be dressed to impress with his drunk ass. He can't out dress me though.

"Open up! This is the one and only, never fake or phony," Church championed, as I buzzed him through the door. He stood barely five and a half feet with an uneven corduroy complexion and Bigen to fill in the patches in his beard. The only person I know cheaper than Turtle is Church. He can squeeze the green out of a dollar. He was dressed in a tailored black blazer with red pinstripes and some Bespoke kicks straight from this spot we like to go to in Detroit.

"What's good? You got my care package in that bag? I'll definitely be crushin' later on tonight," I said anxiously.

"Everything is good, shid' you looking like you got money as long as Reading Road," alleged Church my fast-talking over animated friend with the gift of gab. "Got what you wanted and got something for me."

"We going over Turtle's house tonight,"I warned him.

"What that mean….that nigga told you I better be on my best behavior or else, or something? The truth is he's mad, because he has no sense of humor. You gotta be able to make a woman laugh and cum constantly. That's why he harbors so much animosity towards me. I ain't touched that woman since the last time I touched that woman, and that was before him." Church babbled.

"You drunk already?"

"Not yet, but I feel the spirit coming on," he revealed with a two step. A loud laugh followed as he pulled the already open bottle of Henny, and a few bottles of beers from the slightly torn brown paper bag.

"Hey Craft, look. I got a fourth of a fifth and a half of a six," he professed.

"Church, I'm drivin."

Fuckin with him ain't no tellin what we might run into. Closer to me than some of my family, we've been through some real situations together.

He responded, "I already knew that I took an Uber over here from the hotel. I figured we'd ride out in the Drop and show it off tonight."

The cold air was sneaking in through the breezeway like my Auntie's house in the Village back in the day. I am expecting real good things on the table tonight.

"Where did you get that Atlas statue with the onyx eyes? I never seen one like that before," Church, my brother from another blurted out.

"My home girl sculpted that for me, because of some work I did for her when she was getting started in her career. Her name is Isis. I will introduce you to her sometime this week. We're working on some business now," I informed him.

"Is it business, pleasure or both? I know you nigga. Out of all of us, you stay fucking and fucking up," Church stated, sounding like a hater.

"What the fuck you mean nigga?" I said while checking his temperature and watching his body language in case I had to sock that nigga.

"I'm just saying, you came down here cause you fucked up back home. Your wife threw you out, cause' you kept fucking up," he implied.

28

"How can you of all people make a statement like that, when we were running the streets doing the same shit? I know you ain't hating on my bounce back game? Nigga, she ain't throw me out. She asked me to leave. I left. And that's that," I said angrily. Church stay on some bullshit, but he is who he says he is. Around here, a lot of folks talk don't match their walk.

"You're in your feelings today, big money? I'll be raking in that doe' at the table whether it's cards or bones. I'm in the mood to play some spades and you be reneging. I hope they got some sexy partners who know how to play without jokers," he continued to ramble on.

"O'l joker ass nigga, you better be able to hold your liquor, cause' Turtle might not be the only person ready to whoop that ass."

"I'm feeling lucky tonight. Georgia, Georgia…. Georgia on my mind….," he began to sing off key.

He was living his best life without a care in the world. The windows were cracked. The top was down. You could barely see our heads through the tint. I played this new playlist Ice made for me called "Ride To" a few weeks ago. That woman definitely knows music. I cherish her dearly and hold her in high regard. We've stayed up late many a nights on the phone like high school sweethearts having random discussions ranging from finance, religion, monogamy versus polygamy, and so on. A genuine person over all, I can confide in and vice versa. She's my heart for real, but I got ain't shit ways like my daddy that I don't want to infect her with.

"I'm thinking about quitting drinking like you did, for real, but that's as far as I ever get with it. My blackouts are getting worse and I'm tired of people having to explain my actions to me from the night before. I try drinking less, but the next thing you know I'm either fighting or in jail," Church admitted.

"Jail, when you get locked back up? You be on that reality T.V. shit huh" HAHAHA "This nigga crazy!" I laughed.

"Me and Monica got into it about a week ago, I think she's cheating on me. She be trying to say I think like that, because I'm cheating on her. I just don't trust her. Her DM keep a bubble in it," he said while pausing to take a sip out of his red cup. "The neighbors blew it out or proportion. However, after the second time the police came to the house, they took me down, even though I had the scratches on my neck," Church said, pulling at his collar showing me his scars as proof.

Sadly, I said,"So that's why you're down here to get away from everything for a minute? You will definitely always have a place to stay with me, bruh, you know that. That's why I didn't know why you got a hotel room when I have plenty of room for you to lay your head."

"Appreciate it, but you know how I turn up. I was just respecting the fact that you don't drink no more. As a matter of fact, since we're on the subject, drive by the liquor store, so I can play my number. As soon as I hit, I will give you that $5 dollars I owe you." We both had to laugh at that. Shid', he's had that five dollars a million times over literally before.

"Grab me a pack of gum, my mouth tasting kinda tart," I told him. "I gotta get this dry taste out of my mouth."

"I was going to tell you HAHA. I gotcha stank breath." While he struggled to get out of the car, I placed my hand to my mouth for a breath check. It ain't up to par, but it ain't halitosis either. By the walk, I could tell it was Deidra Corral. She has that one-of-a-kind thickness, small waist trainer waist and curvy hips. Those light green eyes almost like contacts are the perfect hue to compliment her complexion. She has been a regular caller into my show since its inception and I definitely appreciated her support.

The Corral's as a couple have been pillars in the community long before I moved down here. They also frequent those private invitation only parties as well.

"Hey baby," were the first words to roll off the tongue of the fun-sized woman with the enticing hips.

"Deidra, what's going on? You out here getting this money officer? Your husband bet not catch you out here getting your fix. You know the detective don't play that. He's probably watching you right now," I said, knowing it could be true.

"Big head you got an ugly laugh," she said flirtingly while placing her hand on my chest.

"That's the first time I heard that. My pretty words make up for it I'm sure."

"Hmmm. I guess, you smell good and looking good. I know you must taste good, Craft, with your fine ass."

"Deidra, cut that out, for' you get in trouble!"

"I'm just enjoying my view. You know I'm just teasing you. Speaking of trouble, you better holla at your boy Tags. Word on the streets is that he messed around and pulled a move for some freight from the docks. I don't know the specifics, but hopefully, it ain't true and you're not involved," she warned.

"Why would I be involved?" The vibe of the situation turned from all smiles to stone-faced.

"I'm not saying you are, but it's a case my husband is working on. A hit squad from Mexico is here looking to finish ya boy, and baby this is far above my pay grade. I like you, Craft", she rambled on. "If you ain't involved don't get involved."

"I don't know nothing about nothing, Deidra. I'm on my way to this party. I'll see you around. Stay safe beautiful," I said, preparing to leave.

"I most definitely will, baby. You do the same. When is your podcast coming back with new episodes, so I can call in?" Her voice tapered off, and my mind focused, processing the information while heading back to the car.

"While Church went to play his number and probably get some more liquor, I was in the car thinking about a conversation me and Tags had about making a play. It sounded too good to be true, but when he didn't get back with me, I figured it fell through. He said it was legit and I was ready to bite on a 50 percent return on my investment. The times are hard, and everyone's needs more than one hustle. Being busy with this deadline has had me a bit uptight. "A naughty nightcap would do the trick." I said to myself.

"Damn, what took you so long in there Travell?" I intentionally tried to work a nerve and change the subject mentally.

"Man, my momma the only person who can call me that! Trick no good. I'm on my "A" game tonight. Damn! She got ass for days! Ain't that a bitch? Cops putting cuffs on me. How she was touching on you looked like she wanted you to put cuffs on her," Travell spoke with a slight slur.

"Naw, it wasn't like that."

"Well, it wasn't like she was trying to read you your rights either."

"You sound like a chick, nigga," I reminded my homie, not paying him no mind.

A sharp right turn into traffic finally put us on our way to the festivities. Hopefully, he would be sleep soon. This air had late night rendezvous written all over it.

"My girl been blowing me up all day. Craft and I ain't quite ready to sit still yet. Too much running through my mind right now. Let's bend some corners like we used to when we use to steal big momma's car. You remember when she got that switch and tried to whoop you under the couch?"

"Why you always bringing up old shit with your short, big forehead ass?" I joked.

"R.I.P, Big Momma. You beat this nigga into a success like Joe Jackson," he yelled out of the space where the roof used to be.

"I ain't going to be babysitting your drunk ass tonight." I knew no other words to say to the man-sized child whose only beginning to buzz. "You good nigga? You know I was just fucking with you." The look on Church's face turned sour, so I knew something was up.

"I'm straight; small shit to a giant. I been fucked up for a lil' minute. Child support wants my license, Bridgette don't let me see my daughter, bank wants my cars, and a couple of my properties on the brink of foreclosure. Hold up let me finish. I got to gambling and made a few bad investments, and now I'm here trying to get my money back on track. I sold a few of my older renovated properties. I wasn't trying to get back out here in these streets," he admitted.

"I'm literally a phone call away. How much you need?" I asked.

"It ain't about that. You know we've always had a rivalry since we were little. Yeah, I know I can get it from you, but I also know I can get it from me. You done peeped these lenses I got on. I know with your peeping ass. You know these from the "D," and I know you might be quite salty."

"Nigga what the fuck wrong with you? Yeah, them Cardi's decent, but this shit serious."

Travell confessed, "I'm down here to pick up my bounce back. That's another reason I didn't stay over your way either, cause' I didn't want you involved."

Chapter 6

I understood what he was on just by his look. I turned up the music and hit the gas. Rolled through the city with no current destination. I don't know how much time passed. We finally pulled up to a newly redeveloped neighborhood that used to be the projects before gentrification swept in and swept most of the black folks out. I remembered Tyreek's son was one of the last people shot trying to rob a man in broad daylight. The street was newly paved with blacktop and outlined with new paint. Some of the homes were still being constructed. Turtle tried to get me to purchase a lot out here, but I liked how my place was set up.

"Turtle's crib is nice. I see him and Martha ain't doing too bad for themselves, huh Craft?" Church acknowledged, sounding refreshed.

Cars were parked everywhere like the parking lot of a small sports venue. The music was rocking as the sound of festivities could be heard through the brick walls. I'm in the mood for this. The people eating good, laughing, telling jokes or lies; either way the vibe was inviting and friendly. Church was dry when he saw Turtle, but hey, they will work it out one day.

"Hey, Turtle. I see you packed the house tonight. That must be a real nice piece of change you're collecting man," I pryed.

"It's definitely enough to make more with it. Just a heads up, one of Martha's aunts made some dry macaroni that's very light on the cheese. We told folks not to bring nothing, but she insisted on contributing. Make sure you stand clear. You ain't gonna' be roasting me on that show of yours," Turtle said, as we shared that laugh together, because we both knew it was true.

I confronted him, "Hey Turtle. I need to speak to you about that deal. This was supposed to be our collaboration."

"This is a different deal that Martha was able to broker with some people she knows from her sorority. We are still ironing out the kinks from our deal. Don't worry bro, you know I gotcha," he lied, placing his hand on my shoulder. "No sweat. Come in and enjoy yourself. The night is still young," he continued hesitantly, so I knew he was lying. I also knew that I was going to get mines out of this deal regardless.

Church was all off in the corner trying to play nice with some chick whose face I couldn't see, cause' her back is to me. When his head is cocked to the left that's when he's giving what he calls the sermon. Martha and Turtle were smiling and laughing, being cordial for once. I guess that's what a new payday will do. My phone was ringing. It is a call from a private number and that's a no go. I was in the mood for something new. Time to turn the radar on, so I can see what I can see. I don't want anything heavy just a lil conversation for a change. I can get a nightcap later.

"Hey, sugar. I ain't seen you in a while. You've been working out. Let me feel them arms," she flirted.

"I ain't been doing too much. Angie, I see you're still as fine as ever. You the one that's been working out. Do a little twirl , so I can see what your squat life like," I said jokingly.
She began twirling in slow motion . While I held her hand, I couldn't tell if it was squats or a BBL, but it was looking real nice and firm in them jeans.

"You're wearing them jeans, girl," I said licking my lips.

"Thank you, baby. You always know the right things to say," she admitted.

"You make it easy to say, cause it's the truth."

"You hungry? You want me to make you a plate? I know you still like to eat. Them greens made with smoked turkey legs, cause' I know you don't eat pork. Turtle talking about don't bring nothing, but I don't eat everybody's cookin'," she griped, turning her nose up.

"Yeah, put me together a plate with no mac and cheese," I added.

"I hear you got cooking classes once a week over at your place. I didn't even know you be throwing down like that," Angie said curiously.

"Yeah, I can do a lil sumtin sumtin," I smiled.

"Well, why you ain't never cooked for me then," she questioned with a hint of attitude.

"Angie, don't start! you know we too cool. We're like family and I wouldn't want to cross them boundaries," I admitted.

"Mmmmm Hmmm. Whatever, nigga. You must fear all this woman. Turtle know I'm grown. He might be my big brother, but I know what I want," she said seductively.

"Yeah, that's it, Angie! Gone' and make that plate with no mac and cheese please," I urged.

"What's in it for me?" she pressed.

"The fact that you're feeding the hungry should be good enough."

"Oh, I got something you can eat. With your hungry ass," she admitted.

I slapped her on the back pocket of her Lap Kiss jeans while she sashayed away to make my plate. She looked back at me. She was talking with her pussy, and it was all in her eyes. Angie has a high yellow complexion, short curly hair, and a real pretty face. Back in the day we used to call her quarter grand, because of her weight. She probably wasn't quite 250 pounds, but she was close. She always dressed nice and had confidence. Even more so now that she lost 60 pounds. She stood about 5'8, so her frame carried the weight well. I always respected her, cause' she stayed on her grind. An ambitious and nurturing woman is very sexy to me. Several colorful tattoos from Lotus to Koi fish formed a Japanese style mural on her back. She invited me over to play naked twister a few times, but I wasn't trying to go there with her.

I shouted over towards the dining room area, "Hey Turtle, who all downstairs at the table? I'm about ready to take some money." He was all hugged up acting like he couldn't hear me. Fuck'eem. I headed down to feel the cards out. No matter how many times I walked down the stairway, I was impressed with the memorabilia that he collected over the years. From autographed Jerseys to boxing gloves neatly framed and encased in wood and fiberglass.

The smell of that California bud slowly made its way up as I slowly made my way down. Weed used to come in those small yellow envelopes when I was a little boy. Me and my cousins and nem' had to sit on the steps while our parents and the other grown-ups partied. Those Cerwin Vega speakers bumped some of the same music on that playlist Ice made for me. I called her by her assassin name so much sometimes I almost forgot her real name.
Maybe, it's strategic on my part to keep my feelings in check as I danced on the boundaries of her emotional wall.

The large half-moon glass and brass bar was filled with every liquor imaginable and no one was tending it. Greeting those familiar and unfamiliar with either a handshake or a head nod, I made my way to the card table that looked full.

"Dominoes muthafucka!" The small white rectangle with black dots smashed
down onto the green velvet material on the game table.

A voice I'm all too familiar with from the direction on the opposite side of the room said, "This money belongs to daddy."

Tags was over there loud as hell and should have been low-key. Brim and shades on as usual, he stayed dressed up. He probably don't even own a pair of jeans. Cohiba cigar and Blue Label scotch is his go to. He is about 5 years younger than me, but that hustling ass nigga act like a grandpa. As I waived him over and he gestured a finger as if to say hold up. I waived him over again. Finally, relenting, he walked over only as he could with his cigar and drank' in his hand.

"Hold them bones yawl. Gimme a hot minute," Tags shouted to the people at the table.

"I was going to call you tomorrow about that business I was telling you about," he whispered.

"This about some business that ain't my business. Folks coming up to me saying you're hot, cause' of something that went down at the docks," I informed him.

I walked as he followed me out to the pool area. Despite all that laughing and splashing, don't too many people be getting their hair wet. Tracks and Bigen got folks protecting them' roots.

"I'm bringing it to you, 'cause you out here trying to eat like everybody else. I don't want you blindsided," I admitted.

He replied, "You know I keep my game tight. Your information is faulty fam."

"It's just a heads up. They talking about the docks and hitters from Mexico and all types of shit," I repeated what Deidra said.

"Man, I ain't fooled around on them docks in no way shape or form. I deal with paperwork and shit like that. I'm closer to legit now more than I've ever been. Must have been a broad I don't deal with no more, or a nigga of a broad that I do deal with," he objected.

"Just a heads up either way," I cautioned.

"I appreciate the fair one. While we doing each other favors, stay away from that mac and cheese. I don't know who brought that out in public. They should be embarrassed," Tags expressed, tapping my shoulder.

"I already got that warning fam. Nice lookin' though," I laughed.

"They could have warned me," he said while shaking his head in disgust.

Me and Tags kicked it for a few like old times before he went back to playing bones. I stayed out towards the pool chillin' enjoying the sights. I knew he was lying to me, but fuck it. I did my part.

I ain't got nothing to do with it. I gave him the heads up. If that shit was that hot, I can't make no move. No way!

Chapter 7

"I knew you were out here. Why you like being by yourself all the time," Angie implied, walking towards me with a nice plate.

"Thank you for the plate. Everything looks good. I enjoy being by myself in healthy doses not on no secluded weird uncle in the room shit," I laughed as the words tapered off.

"You need to do stand up. You're funny as hell and keep me laughing," she suggested, smiling.

" Naw, I be serious. You just think it's funny. These greens bangin!" I mumbled with a mouth full of food tasting a familiar flavor.

"I seasoned them with Gold Label. You did your thang with that seasoning blend. I bought a spicy and a regular blend online," Angie spoke, evoking pride.

Extremely grateful, I confessed ,"Thanks for your support and helping me establish my brand."

"You're more than welcome," she said.

"How is your son doing? Is he still playing football?" I asked as I caught her staring at that thick print in my pants.

She continued without missing a beat, "He's staying with his dad. He didn't want to play sports suddenly and started wanting to run the streets and talk back. Hopefully, his dad will get him together, cause' I don't want him out here in these streets."

"I can feel that. He has enough talent and intelligence to do anything he wants even if he doesn't play sports. My homeboy has programs down at the REC that can hopefully peek his interest. It's available at multiple locations, and transportation and food are provided. I'mma text you the information," I told her.

"Thank you, boo. I appreciate it," Angie remarked softly.

My phone began to ring from an anonymous number again. I ignored it like the last time, but I should have blocked it the first time. "Who calling you this late? These almost booty call hours, and you're coming home with me tonight. I've been thinking about you ever since you came in the door," Angie exaggerated.

"I got plans after I leave here tonight. Plus, I got Church with me," I replied.

"Church grown as hell. He up there playing cards with one of Martha's cousins. He might be leaving you by yourself tonight," she assumed slowly walking towards me as if she was trying to steal a kiss.

I grabbed her gently by the wrist momentarily covering up the tattoo of her ex's name. "You're my homeboy's sister and I don't want to hurt you."

"How you know I won't be the one that hurts you?" she admitted as we stared intently into each other's eyes.

"I don't, but with odds like that, it don't sound like it's worth it at all," I countered.

Angie acted like she needed to spend 25 hours a day with me. I don't do clingy, but she smelled good and looked good. Made me want to put a passion mark on her booty.

She continued, "I'm grown. I can handle whatever you can bring. You got my number. I will be leaving in a few. It ain't no rush. I know Turtle and them party all night. I'm by myself this weekend and I want your company. When you're done here, no matter what time, call me if you' coming through."

She grabbed my half-eaten plate and folded it like a taco, and put it in the trash as she headed upstairs. I be trying to bury that side of me. Her eyes spoke for her pussy again and I understood every word. I don't know what's up with me. It's usually a "yeah" or "no". Is Turtle the fact I got Church with me or something else? I must've gotten a contact, cause' I was trippin.

Chapter 8

My phone rang. This time it was a number and a face that I'm trying to spend time with. "Hey, Stormy. How are you doing, baby?"

"I'm exhausted, needing a massage and some quality time with my best friend," she said.

"I'm at Turtle's right now. I didn't think you would be in town for a few days."

"I know, but I miss you, so I cut my business trip short, cause' we got a lot of making up to do," Stormy expressed.

"You need to be making up with me," I said.

"I'm sorry, babe. Sometimes, I just get to acting all crazy. You make me like that. It ain't got nothing to do with sex. I love how I know you and you know me," she confessed.

"Stormy, that don't have nothing to do with nothing. You really was on some bullshit."

"I know…. It won't happen again," she paused, "I will pay to get your truck window fixed."

"It bet not happen again, cause' my cut off game better than my dick game."

"Don't act like that! You know you love me."

"Yeah, I love you, but I love me more. I don't want no love where respect ain't first, and no pussy that don't come with peace."

"I said, I'm sorry. What time you coming home? I can be showered and waiting for you," Stormy asked.

"It's going to be a minute. I'm chillin'. Cook them metts and that chili. I want some coney metts when I get there. Don't touch my Grippo's I shook it, so I know it's a good bag," I instructed.

"You know it's too late to be eating like that."

"You ain't complaining when I'm eating you late like that, girl. Get in that kitchen and get it done!"

"OK, baby," she agreed.

"I bought them metts and stuff for us. Damn Stormy tore the big boy truck up," said the grown toddler laughing and talkin at the same time.

"Church, how long your ear hustling ass been standing there? You ain't the only one going through some thangs bruh," I admitted.

"That shit light. You go through shit in relationships. I'm finna' head out with my newfound spades partner. We're headed back to my room. I will get atcha' sometime in the afternoon. I know Stormy ain't finna' let you out.

Yawl making up all weekend," Church's tipsy ass said, grinning while rubbing his palms together like Birdman.

"Whatever! Don't make that run without hollering at me first."

"That ain't till Sunday. I'm good. You be worrying too much bruh. I'll get atcha'. I thought you was leaving with Angie. You getting plates and shit made," Church joked.

"Shid, Angie was showing some love," I said, downplaying it.

"I noticed you ain't have none of that dry ass mac. My spade partner momma made it. She can play some cards, but she ain't look out for a nigga on that mac at all. Now I gotta take it out on her. HAHA!" Church laughed.

"Everybody ain't got it like Craft," I smirked, partially exposing my pearly whites.

"Nigga, I taught you," said the lying drunken master. My hand itching. I guess I'll try my luck on them cards since my babysitting duties are over for now. Something about this deal ain't sitting right with me. Tags perpin' trying to out maneuver me, he can keep that heat over that way. Stormy gonna have to wait. She owe down anyway. As far as Angie, she really is a temptress," he thought while walking to the card table.

Chapter 9

Counting my money, I realized I tore they asses up. I was ahead ten bands which is a good day. But of course, if anyone would ask, I lost five bands and I ain't got it to give. One of them sore losers at the table might blurt out I won, but I kept my private life separate for the most part. I took my phone off do not disturb, because there's no interruptions when I'm gambling. If it was a real emergency, they can call me direct at Turtle's house. It was about six something and the sun was still asleep on this side of the world. There were a few familiar cars left belonging to faces. I battled for days before barely washing up. There was a back and forth rumble until either fatigue, the cards, or lack of money determined the true winner.

That last hand of four queens and a king resonated with me. It reminded me of a story my uncle told me as a child. I was sitting on his orange and black plaid couch with the broken zipper exposing the yellowish orange cushion. Empty beer cans overflowed and tried to crawl out of the trash like crabs in a barrel.

While shuffling his worn deck of cards, he asked me, "Neph, what is your favorite king in the deck?"

"The King of Spades," I replied eagerly waiting for the magic to unfold.

He shuffled the cards and gave a few quick cuts. He flipped the top card face up and revealed the King of Spades in all of his splendor.

"The King of Spades is the most powerful king. He's the King Maker. He possesses charm, wisdom, wealth and omnipotent power," he explained, putting me up on game. Another shuffle of the cards and the Queen of Diamonds was revealed. "She is a special queen, beautiful in a way only she could be. But wealth is her first love and she will always cost you more than you will receive. She comes to your castle bearing gifts disguised as a damsel in distress. You combat her with wit. If not, she will be sure to take you for all you have," he said calmly.

Flipping the next card, he continued, "The Queen of Clubs, she is seductive and entertaining, and able to make your wildest fantasies come true. She is like nightlife and orgies with seductive perfumes. "No is not a response for her, if yeah means more to you," he continued. You deal with her with charm and avoid her from charming you," he taught.

I listened intently as the halos around his cataracts seemingly rotated and glowed. His brown dental partial exposed his gold canine tooth. The bridge made of cards came neatly down together in his hands as he revealed the next queen to me waiting for me to instruct him.

He further explained, "The Queen of Hearts is loving and soft. Her strength is in her femininity. She occupies your mind and seduces your soul with love. But beware, combat her with power. For your love for her will weaken you."

He split the deck in half. No shuffle from the riverboat gambler this time. The two stacks sat seemingly evenly parted on the wooden table with the round, water stains. Before I could reach to pick a card, he pulled the hidden Queen of Spades from behind my head.

"She is the Queen of Queens. She possess all of the strengths that the other queens have, but she is the reflection of her king, in charm, wisdom, wealth and power. How do I defend against her then," I asked as if the riddle had stomped me." He continued, "Be patient, for she is you. You sacrifice the Queen to protect the King!"

Chapter 10

Looking at my phone, I saw a lot of blocked interruptions during my winning spree. Damn, Angie hit me up like she wouldn't have let me leave if I came over.

11:30 p.m.
Angie: I'm home.

12:25 a.m.
Angie: WYD? Eggplant, peach, water emojis.

01:03 a.m.
Angie: I'm still up waiting.

01:45 a.m.
Angie: Hello?

02:48 a.m.
Angie: I guess you decided to do something else???

"Angie and I will definitely have to keep it professional. I have too much business to handle to be tied down. This is my first weekend of pure leisure in months, and I'm not spending time doing anything, but what makes me smile," I said, talking to myself.

02:53 a.m.
Church: I made it to the room.

02:55 a.m.
P.R.O.D. I forgot to remind him to hit me up.

03:05 a.m.
Dick: Call me later today. Those numbers are looking favorable. We can set up a meeting in a day or two to go over the paperwork.

"Yes! I can make this move with Isis worthwhile. I gotta hit the gym real hard starting Monday. Ain't no sense in lying to myself this weekend is for turn up only" I said.

03:33 a.m.
Stormy: Good luck on them cards, baby. You ain't here yet, so you must be winning.

"HAHA. She knows me too well," I said, thinking a loud.

03:43 a.m.

Ice: You crossed my mind. I'm worried about
        you. Call me when you get a minute.

    "What Ice talking about now," I said in anguish. Church left his bag with a corner of liquor in the bottle on the passenger side. I ain't gonna do Turtle and nem' yard like that, but I'm tossing it the first chance I get.

    "Ice," I commanded my automatic dial system, "Good morning beautiful, did I wake you up?"

    "Good morning. No, you didn't," she immediately responded after she yawned. "You must have done good on the table, cause' you're in a good mood."

    "Naw, I'm down 5 bands. They got off on me early. I tried to win it back, but it just wasn't my night. Your message seemed urgent. What's going on?" I inquired.

    "I've known you for too long. You won something, probably those five bands you say you lost. I ain't trying to see if I can hold something," Ice replied.

"You know you could hold it, if you want to," I laughed, "What's up girl?"

"It's too early for being nasty," she said.

"It ain't nothing like dessert for breakfast."

"Boy you so….," she giggled.

I tossed the bag in an undeveloped area. As I peeled off, the bottle came crashing down with a smash. "What was that noise?" Ice asked.

"Oh, I was getting rid of some trash. Now what was' you saying baby?"

"Your nasty butt made me lose my train of thought. I've been feeling you a lot lately," she admitted.

"At the shop, you just told me you would never give me the time of day," I said with a smirk.

"No, seriously. I don't know what you got yourself into, or what you're finna' get into, but you better be careful. The storm waters are on the horizon, and that castle built on sand will soon fall," she warned.

"What the fuck does that mean, Shanice? I don't need this right now," I said angrily. Damn, I guess I do remember her real name, I said surprisingly to myself.

"Calm down, Jont'e. This knowledge is on my spirit, and I had to share it with you.

Hopefully, you're in a position to avoid whatever it might be," Ice replied.

"You ain't telling me nothing but riddles. You know I ain't in these streets!" I quickly replied. "I know, but you have one foot in just like everyone you surround yourself with. You might not do it yourself, but you don't mind investing in certain things that are street related. You keep your yard clean, but you don't mind trashing someone else's, if you can make a buck or two," she said. I looked around as if she was watching me before I began my denial.

"That ain't true. I'm trying to eat and live as comfortable as possible," I said, keeping it a buck.

"I capalized on various opportunities, but that's about it."

"That Drop, a.k.a "your pretty, black, bitch" and that penthouse you could have bought without Tags doing what he does best. You have more than enough money. It is because of your dealings in the darkness that I haven't moved forward on our barbershop and salon venture," she finally revealed.

"Sometimes, I find refuge in this so-called darkness. It's like the shade from the heat," I responded.

"I'm not one of your poems you can edit if you don't like the flow. Anytime you come to the shop, whether you're late for an appointment, or don't have an appointment, I'm happy to see you. Anytime I cut your hair and shave you, I pray that you be safe. You've talked in your sleep on more than one occasion while you were having nightmares, or life confirmations." Ice revealed.

"Where is all of this coming from?" I interrupted.

"We spoke in great lengths about this. We talked about your grandmother, even though she dealt with mental illness. She was instrumental in your upbringing, and also simply by being able to speak life into you," Ice said caringly.

"I don't want to hear this shit right now! You know how I am about my grandma," I said as I abruptly pulled over to the edge of the road. I ignored the person behind me honking their horn and probably flipping me off.
Ice was still talking, but I couldn't seem to hear anything, but the cadence of my hazard lights.

Chapter 11

"Jont'e! Craft! Hey baby, are you there?" The wind whispered and screamed frantically demanding a response. I removed my tinted lenses and threw them down in the empty seat next to me, hoping to hear her better while gathering myself. After a brief intermission, "Yeah, I'm here," I responded finally ready to face my fears.

"You have old doors you need to close and dead relationships that you need to let go of. You have made men kings and they resent you for it," Ice said.

"Who resents me for making them a king? Anything I do is out of love. I don't be on no remember when I did that for you, or you owe me type shit," I insisted.

"Your license plate says what?" she snarled.

"King Maker spelled K-1-N-G M-K-R,"I said.

"So how is it that you want peace and you prove your vanity loud and clear? How are you acting like you didn't know that the very kings you made wouldn't try to tear your castle down? We both know by Kingmaker you mean deity.

Let me tell you this, in terms of kings you have positioned, females are included too," Ice disclosed.

"Are you directly a part of this bullshit, and what man would settle for being a king if he can be greater than a king? I consider myself more of a teacher or mentor," I responded.

"I love you with all of my soul, and to answer your questions, hell no! You mean too much to me on levels that I have never experienced before and levels we have yet to experience together. Any man wanting to exalt himself that high should know that he has enemies in his wake constantly," Ice lectured.

"You sounding like a poet your damn self with all that script. But keep going tho'. HAHA!," I laughed.

"You can't never be serious. This ain't no game!" she argued.

"I'm very aware of the seriousness of this situation. Sometimes I joke to numb myself of the reality of my past. I always hated when my mother would call me a Deacon. As brilliant as I am, how could she not see me as a Reverend at the minimum. Shid, fuck it, the Pope, God damn it," I said with rage in my spirit.

Ice interjected, "Your momma ain't got nothing to do with this."

"I'm not saying she does; however, because of that, I knew when I had children one day I would tell them they could be the best of anything they put their minds to," I said.

"You would make a great father," Ice confessed.

"I'm saying that I had to see me as the best. I don't walk around like I think I'm better than anyone. I just know I'm not less than anyone. People will call me arrogant, because I have more confidence in myself than they think I should. They had the choice to choose the King Maker moniker, but everybody wants to be kings. I shared that story with you before regarding me being the first person in the house to have a bed that no one gave to me, or a bed that couldn't be taken away from me from a rental place. I grew up sleeping on pallets on the floor, used bags of clothes as pillows, sheets as curtains, and curtains as sheets depending on the time period. Who the FUCK am I supposed

to be? Why would I want to live that life again, eviction notices on the door. Furniture sat out so all the kids can see it as we came home from school. My past taught me to be the best I can be, and the best I can be is The King Maker. I won't apologize for who I am destined to be. I'm unable to rewrite history, but I be damn if I don't break the cycle," I insisted.

The phone was silent. I looked at my dash to make sure the call was still connected. I was heated as well as relieved, as if a burden had been lifted off my shoulders. Atlas, no longer condemned to hold up the sky.

"Shanice, baby are you still there?" I asked.

"Yes, I'm here," she wimpered.

"What's wrong? Are you crying?" I asked genuinely concerned.

"No," she answered.

I ignored her answer and asked, "What you crying for?"

"I'm scared that you traded heaven for a crown. I haven't been asleep and I've been praying for you all night." Ice admitted.

"It ain't nothing you need to be afraid of. I ain't into nothing babe," I promised.

"It is because of who you are, more than anything you did." Ice revealed.

Them poker face muthafuckas gonna have to have a hell of a hand, and they better know how to play it too. I want to crush my enemies. I put my shades on as the sun began to peak its head, and covered up my copper colored eyes. "I'm on my way over babe," I finally spoke.

"Do you have your key with you, or do you need me to unlock the door?" Ice asked.

"I have my key, baby. I just need you to make me some tea. You know how I like it," I said.

"You try it with cinnamon in it yet?" Ice replied.

That's who suggested that cinnamon to me. This morning is full of revelations. "Naw baby, I haven't, but it's a pinch of cinnamon kind of day. I'm 20 minutes away."

Chapter 12

I cranked up the music like Rocky while "Eye of the Tiger" played, "My engine roared down the highway as if that building on the west side was going to disappear if I didn't get there. "Tinted lenses behind tinted windows. Blowing smoke in the clouds while feeling the wind blow. Fuck holding back tears, I'd rather let the tears flow. Tinted lenses behind tinted windows. Blowing smoke into the wind while feeling the wind blow. Fuck holding back tears, I'd rather let the tears flow." It was "Tinted Windows" by Diamond King on repeat the whole way.

The three- floor, six- family apartment building that I had converted into three nice size lofts was a hell of a deal. Ice occupied the first floor. The basement was once occupied by one of my original tenants before she moved in with her son during renovations, never to return. It will be a small daycare center once I get Tags to get the proper paperwork for me. Scratch that, he ain't to be trusted. This business will be established without him. The top floor is my getaway when I'm too busy, or too tired to make it back to the penthouse.

This will be a short visit. My schedule is hectic today. Ice has clients at the shop and Stormy is waiting on me to finally come in. The partially manicured bushes surrounding the property are almost in need of a trim. The faded mulch needs to be redone as well. I parked the drop next to her bright pink Jeep, I made my way up the few flight of stairs with a tired light jog.

The smell of breakfast cooking in the hallway enticing my nose, I turned my key. As I walked up behind her into an apartment that was full of life. I saw plants with leaves shaped like hearts, or spades depending on the way you looked at them. There were large clay pots that she made herself when she took those one classes. A 75-gallon aquarium with salt-water fish sat under the African masks that she picked up from some thrift store.

There was a birdcage, with no door. It was for birds she never got. It symbolically swung by the open window near the back hallway. That same window where I held her from behind and shared my vision with her on turning this building into a salon, barber, and massage parlor, respectively, on each floor. I planted soft kisses in the heart shaped tattoo on her neck that's missing my initials.

"Ooh, you scared me," said the petite curvy woman with the blue and yellow maize color short shorts on. "I started breakfast. I figured you might be hungry. A Cajun turkey, egg white omelet with avocado, grits and some of my specially diced potatoes that you like," Ice said proudly.

"Thanks, baby. I don't have much of an appetite. I can't stay long. I have a lot to do today," I reminded her.

"You got enough time to eat some of this food. Go ahead and make yourself comfortable. I will bring you your tea shortly," she insisted.

I made my way to her butter soft, mustard yellow leather couch, I tossed a few of the extra decorative pillows out of my way. Freed my feet from my shoes. Emptied my pockets. Placed 4 of the 10 thousand dollars and my keys in the middle of the chessboard, and knocked over the king in the process. Awakened by the smell of cinnamon from the hot tea, she presented to me. "You were snoring louder than usual. You might have sleep apnea," she warned.

"You're a doctor and a fortune teller now?" I said jokingly.

"I can be whatever you need me to be, and you know I will be it very well," Ice replied.

That statement aroused me for some reason. Maybe, it's because I'm horny, or because her words were true. She motioned for me to sit up momentarily, so I could lay my slightly elevated head on her. Right between her thighs and her stomach. The nipple jewelry on her handful size breasts seemed to be looking right at me through her white cotton tank top.

"I'm starting to get my appetite, but it ain't for an omelette," I implied.

Her house smelled of cleanliness: everything arranged in order, not with a chemical smell, but as if fresh air circulated often. Her place was meant to be lived in. The couches weren't covered in plastic like my aunts white couch used to be. My zone was intensified with the awakening of my taste buds.

"Here," Ice gestured with a sample of everything on the fork. Feeding me and her from the same plate, she took turns as if she was sharing her last. The food was good. I could taste the Gold Label all in them' eggs.

"This food taste like my cooking classes have paid off in a major way. You're welcome," I said in jest.

71

"Please. You gave me some pointers, I can't lie, but my momma been throwing down in the kitchen my whole life," she corrected.

"I've tasted some food you brought from your momma house. That gravy tasted like it was instant over that hard rice. HAHA!" I laughed.

"You always cappin'. It was good to me," Ice rebutted.

"And you're good to me, Ice. Definitely someone who genuinely has my back and best interest at heart. Sometimes, I'm moving so fast that I don't take out the necessary time to acknowledge how important you are to my professional success and personal sanity. I sincerely appreciate you," I revealed.

"I know you do. You're just stubborn, and don't want to listen to nobody," she interjected.

"There you go killin' the vibe," I said.

"No, I'm not, but my dreams and intuition are real. It's a negative storm charging, and I want you to be mindful baby that's all," Ice said lovingly.

I lifted my head from her lap at the seriousness of her words. I was not really in the mood to discuss war strategies with her. My mind raced a million miles a minute and I thought if I changed the subject it would slow things down.

Chapter 13

"You got some food on your lip. Let me get it," I teased. Stealing a kiss, I removed what was never there while I uncovered what always was.

"Craft, stop it, you play too much!" she said, pretending to reject me.

"I want some dessert," I admitted seriously with a look talking with my dick.

A burst of energy rushed into me. The anxiety of best friends becoming lovers had fallen by the wayside. I sat the half-eaten plate of food on the other end of the coffee table. Ice, the aggressor, peeled me from the clothes that smelled of smoke and victory. Her lips transported kisses all over my body until she positioned herself in front of my erection. She used a stray pillow under her knees to comfort her foundation, and unzipped my pants with her teeth. Her defenses were unable to guard her nature any longer.

She freed my dick like a caged lion. Kissed it shyly and sucked on it slow with the intentions to make me erupt in her mouth. She briefly held my manhood firmly and exposed her green shellac nails. Then she gripped the cushions of the couch like handlebars while she moaned and tasted my full flavor.

"Put it in the back of your throat," I commanded with a whisper.

Ice obliged by taking me in further, double tapping her tonsils gagging slightly. With watery eyes, her confidence took over and she put her hands on my hands. She glided her head up and down to a song only she could hear. The poppin sound she made with her mouth on the head of my dick curled my toes as my phone rang. I looked at the phone and closed my eyes not even remembering who it was. Somewhere in between heaven and the unknown is where my mind drifted.

Ready to put my hardness inside of her soul, I motioned her to get up. She looked me directly in my eyes and in defiance she closed her eyes and continued sucking and making love to me with her mouth. We were playing chess on a different kind of board. Her every move tried to get me to submit to her will, but I knew better than that. Finally, ready to feel me inside of her, she stepped out of her wet shorts and bent over the couch. Her soaked thighs were evidence of the pleasure she received while she pleasured me. I placed the head of my dick at the doorway of her pussy.

"Be gentle," were the last words she spoke before I made full contact with her soul. I knocked on her door a few times. It caused the piercing in her clit to swing in the wind before her tight wet pussy gave way to my advances. Every thrust was gentle enough to make her grip the top of the couch with one hand. With her other arm stretched back like a relay racer, she attempted to guide my depth with the other hand. I secured both of her wrists in my palms like hand cuffs and began penetrating her essence. My balls and my erection tore down her house of cards. My rhythm drummed on her soul. My soundtrack played in her head while she announced orgasm after orgasm. We were Gods in the flesh creating a gospel on our own frequency. I grabbed her thighs, so there was nowhere to run as the feelings intensified.

"This pussy belongs to me," I thrusted with no neighbors to share the news with. "Who pussy is it?" I asked already knowing the answer.

"Yours, Jont'e. Yours," she screamed again while looking back at me in ecstasy.

I came to reign and conquer as I crushed her city with every blow. Pussy juices like morning dew splashed on my six-pack. I hit my target consistently with pinpoint accuracy and caressed the ridges of her G-spot. I climbed the stairway to heaven in her pussy. Jerking while inviting me further inside of her, I touched the bottom of her mixing bowl with every stroke. I scraped the juice like cake batter from her walls.

She fucked back using the top of the couch to strengthen her position with every dip of her body and turning of her hips. I began grinding back like Reggae night on the dance floor. I switched positions with her on top going from the snake charmer to being charmed by the snake. Her grapefruits rattled in the air as she salsa danced on top of me. She placed my head in her hands and went in for the kill looking me directly in the eyes. Her tongue sandwiched between her teeth in between kisses. Her eyes rolled into the back of her head as her gyrating body began to clinch. My big toes were standing at full attention while my other toes gracefully bowed down. She covered my mouth to muffle me. Our bodies echoed. I gripped her shoulders and thrust upward from the center of my soul.

"Cum in me," she whispered while her pussy rubbed against my Genie lamp. Granting her wish, I released myself inside of her. Her sultry dance continued as the passion deepened. She came one final time on my upward thrust. Her body shuttered and came to a sudden rest on top of me. She bursted into tears as she began crying on my shoulder. I held her without ceasing, and comforted her soul. My shoulders and chest were her refuge from the storm. Half hard and still inside of her, I kept her safe in my arms. I was dripped with sweat, winded and relieved. As I looked at my watch, I saw that me and time weren't on the same page.

"Shit I gotta go!" I yelled.

"I know you gotta leave. Just stay a few more minutes," Ice spoke in broken whimpering words.

"Baby I gotta…." I attempted to say.

"Please just a little bit more. My legs are still shaking and I can still feel you inside of me. I will get a rag and wash you off baby. Just a few more minutes," she spoke, teeth chattering.

Chapter 14

Against my better judgment, I remained inside of her. We began kissing and picking right up where we left off. Several missed calls later, my marathon came to an exhausting end. I stood at attention while she wiped me down with a hot rag. This gave me time to go through the messages on my phone. Stormy called an hour ago and left several messages regarding getting breakfast from Big Barbs. I worked up an appetite, but I needed to hit the shower and get dressed. I kissed her as I was already halfway out the door.

"You must don't have many heads to cut today," I stated noticing the time.

"I took the first half of the day off. You were more important. I didn't know how today would play out, and I wanted to make sure I had the time for you," she replied. "We ended up having almost too much time on our hands," I laughed.

"I enjoyed every minute of it too!" she admitted.

"I know you did. You're a veteran on the low," I said with a wink.

"My abstinence didn't kill my competitive spirit. Today, felt so right. If you get time with your busy self, call me later," she smiled.

"OK, later, baby. Oh, put them few dollars up for me," I reminded her. Abstinence or not, that was banging. I'm glad I finally pulled the trigger on that. I waited till' I was well on my way to the house before calling Stormy. I tried to cut into some of my delayed responses.

"Stormy, what's up baby?" I asked to check her temperature.

"Where you at?" she inquired.

"I'm on my way to grab some food from Big Barbs," I lied.

"I didn't want to do carryout. I wanted to sit in and relax. What took you so long to respond?"she continued. "I already know you ain't been over Turtle's. I already called to make sure you were still alive,"she said angrily.

"I was riding around clearing my head. I stopped at my building on the west side for a minute and fell asleep," I responded quickly.

"Yeah, you fell asleep alright. Probably fell asleep in some pussy!" she snapped.

"Don't you start!" I commanded gritting my teeth.

"I'm gonna finish. I'm smelling your lying ass dick when you get here," she yelled angrily.

"Here we go again. You bet not be on no bullshit, cause' you can take your ass home," I told her.

"I'm going home alright. Let me find out that dick ain't smelling right," she promised.
"This dick smelling like it supposed to smell, like I need to get in the shower. You want something from Big Barbs still or what?" I said calmly.

"My appetite ain't coming back till you comeback and I make sure that dick kosher, so I might as well wait till after you get here," Ice said sternly.

"Aight later." It is what it is. Disconnecting the call, I put my shades on and lit my cigar and headed to my next storm. I have to reevaluate my life. I'm looking like a storm chaser out here.

Chapter 15

"Ding!" Who texting me?

11:15 a.m.

Angie: Turtle said you left about 7 hours ago
          after you won all the money. Let me
          hold something, big money. LOL. You
          could have at least texted me back to
          let me know something.

"Ding!"

11:16 a.m.

Angie: Why you keep reading my messages
          and not responding? Give me a call or
          stop through. I'm in the mood to play
          which hole feels the best tonight.
          TTYL ?

"Damn, she got my kneecaps hard. HAHAHA!
Turtle better get his sister." I headed into the
house to weather the storm with Stormy, Ice's
scent on my mustache. We crossed boundaries
that we have been tempting with for years. We
became closer over the years after that
miscarriage, that I believe was an abortion that

Stormy had. I wasn't ready for a baby, neither was she. We were so career-minded and focused on our money. She was expanding her brand. I was perfecting my hustle and the time just never seemed perfect.

She told me that she began bleeding heavy through her clothes, and the baby came out in the toilet while she was 6 or 7 weeks. She was living in Los Angeles at the time. That was about a year before she moved to be closer to me. I offered to fly there, or she could fly to me, but she said she needed time to herself. That time alone didn't stop her from seeing clients and doing anything business related. On more than one occasion, I've accused her directly to her face even though I didn't have any proof. Most times, I don't feel guilty for it either.

"Beep! Beep!" My bad, I gestured through the top of my car. I was in deep thought at the green light. Folk got places to go and I still hadn't gotten any sleep yet. Tired, but not sleepy. I knew things would never be the same between me and Ice whether for the good, or for the bad. I wondered if she would try to spend more time on a sexual tip instead of the inadvertent flirting like we did on so many occasions. Ice and I have slept together in the same bed multiple times either at my place, at her spot, or even at the penthouse, but no matter what we never had sex.

We watched movies and ate snacks. We behaved almost like children, as we had fun and laughed. It felt so right. It was like a transferring of spirits type of deal like Big I was saying, but I never picked up bad vibes with her at all. I'm surprised Church ain't hit me up yet. It's about noon and he is probably laid up, hungover, or talking bout he wasn't getting out till late. He ain't gonna believe the night I had. I'm sure Stormy got something work related to do, so we won't be chilling too long. We will probably spend most of the daylight together into the early night, and then she will be in for the night. Being a homebody has always been her thang when she wasn't working.

Ice is the same way, but our interactions are more peaceful. Me and Stormy's are well... stormy. They have a lot of similarities, but then they are like night and day. I'm sure Ice will give me a call later. As a matter of fact, I will wait until she calls me to give her a chance to get situated. I finally arrived at the Penthouse. The patio door was open which filled the house with fresh air and sunshine.

I could tell Stormy had been there meddling with my stuff; which is what she calls cleaning up. The kitchen and living room area had been thoroughly cleaned. The last time she called herself cleaning up, she threw the tickets away to a play that I got for us from Tags on the low. Bedroom cleaned, new linen, and comforter was her ritual. One time, she came in calling herself searching for stains on my sheets. I will slide in the shower while she is away. All of that fussing and accusations and she ain't even here right now. The door opened, and I jumped in the shower putting soap on my private region. I didn't have time to grab a rag as Stormy came busting in.

"Why you jump in the shower before I got here to check your dick?" Stormy screamed.

"I just started. You can smell it right now, or my draws are over there. You can smell them. What? Am I supposed to wait for your permission," I said matter of factly.

"It sounded like the water started running when I was coming in the house and you know I ain't sniffing your funky ass draws!" Stormy yelled.

"I'm not sure when you came in, babe. I see you got your nails painted my favorite color.

They look good," I admitted, trying to change the subject.

"Yeah, I should have gotten a different color with your lying ass. Every time I see a chick with green nail polish I be thinking it's one of your hoes," Stormy accused.

"Girl, I don't fuck with hoes. Baby, just get in the shower with me, so I can show you how much I missed you," I gestured.

"You couldn't've missed me that much. Your ass was out all night," she snarled.

"I won a couple of bands, but you knew that, cause' you talked to Turtle," I said.

"Turtle said you won all of the money. We both know it was more than two. How much was it?" she demanded.

"Shid, about three for real. It wasn't that heavy last night. We was going back and forth on some gladiator shit," I lied.

"You starting to lie too much lately. Turtle said about ten stacks, cause' you was bragging counting your money. You know his big mouth ass gonna tell me everything, cause' he fake like me. Yuck! With his funny built ass . You always being cocky. When will you learn that power is silent too," Stormy said, pretending to be an expert.

85

Cutting my shower short, I stepped out onto the heated the floors. I thrust my feet into my slides and head over to Stormy.

"Don't be using my towel. Where is yours at with your friendly dick ass?" she complained.

"This dick is only friendly to you, baby. Come and smell it," I said waiving her over.

"Boy, you know that black soap too strong. I can't smell nothing from yesterday except that stanky cigar on your breath. You probably smoked that to cover up the pussy smell. If you been out this long, I know whoever it was had a toothbrush for your nasty ass," she argued.

I grabbed her instantly. She put up a little fight before giving in to me. I lifted up her skirt and there were no panties underneath. "A beautiful day to let this pussy breath," I said kissing her freshly waxed pussy with my tongue.

"Baby, it's been too long. I want to feel you," she moaned.

Ignoring her request, I began tasting her nectar, and drinking from her endless river. I flicked my tongue like a lion seeing my reflection in the ripples. She was like a pretty, bright pink, ripe fruit releasing its juices with every caressing touch. I applied soft kisses and slurps on her clitoris while she gripped her thighs

86

intently. A scent and flavor uniquely her own drove me to plant my face deep inside of her. Ambrosia in her chalice, she poured infinitely from her tree of life. Her legs spread eagle. She welcomed me in to share the freedom of her nest. I placed a passion mark on her inner thigh near the tattoo of my name. Nibbling on her plump round breast; her firm nipples extended.

"I love you," she rejoiced to me in ectasy. Biting on her bottom lip, she moaned, "Please put it in. I want to feel you!"

Chapter 16

It's been weeks since I've been inside of her. Starting off slow in missionary with kisses and whispers, I explored her world like I had never been there before. Her pussy muscles clinched and released me in rhythm.

"Deeper, deeper," she commanded me in a voice so gentle.

My raw manhood began swelling more while her words spoke to my soul. I scraped the bottom of her good, wet pussy in search for the buried treasure. She wrapped her legs around me, her fingernails scratched the surface of my skin every time I touched bottom realigning her chakras.

"Where that treasure at in this pussy, huh? Where that treasure at?" I demanded an answer.

"It's right here!" Her words echoed from a place deep down in her soul. My dick transformed into a golden shovel breaking new ground with every deep stroke.

"Right there, baby! Oh, right there!" Stormy's soul continued to echo, as it bounced off the walls and through the open doors. I was a pirate looking for the treasure that belonged to me.

She screamed, "Harder baby, harder baby! I'm coming! AHHHH. Shit, I'm coming!"

Slow deep strokes, then firm deep strokes made her melt like wet clay. "Turn over," I demanded.

"Yes, punish me! I've been a bad girl," she yelled.

I rubbed the tip of my erection on the lips of her pussy, and teased her. As I tempted her, I spit in between her booty cheeks before inserting my thumb in her ass. I continued with slow constant strokes as she rocked back and forth guiding my dick and my thumb deeper inside of her. She didn't want mercy; punishment pleasured her soul. Every dig with the magic shovel revealed different levels of treasure. I grinned slyly in pleasure as she gripped the sheets and rested her head sideways on the bare mattress. Pulling my dick from inside of her, I placed it in her mouth. She is a fan of her nectar just as I am, so she sucked me slowly and lovingly .

I playfully smacked her in the face with my erection before putting it in her back door. The final course of the buffet was a chocolate éclair. I gave her deep strokes like she liked. Pulled her hair like she liked. She is a freak like I like. She was cummin' simultaneously out of her ass and her pussy. I pumped ferociously and tried to knock the bottom out. My hands were firmly around her neck completely covering the heart shaped tattoo with my initials. I finished up last. I was exhausted with a light leg cramp, but I laid face up smiling in the winner's circle.

Chapter 17

On our way to Big Barbs, I finally grabbed something to eat. It was about 1:30 p.m. and time had completely gotten away from me.

"I know you trying to just spend the earlier part of the day with me. Then you're doing your thang like always," she said angrily.

"I got a late start today. You know I have deadlines and business with Church to deal with. Can we at least make it through the day before you start trippin?" I said calmly.

"Oh, I'm not trippin. Go ahead and enjoy yourself. Me and my girls having a girl's night out tonight, so it's cool. Don't wait up," Stormy warned.

"Don't wait up? Who the fuck you think you talking to?" I said, meaning every word.

"Your bipolar ass need a check. You know I was just playing," she responded, attempting to redact her statement.

"I know if I did get a check, you wouldn't be my payee," I said jokingly.

"I know your momma ain't gonna be it either, cause' yo ass a' be wet. HAHAHA," she laughed.

I interrupted, "Don't get on my momma. What about your old thotty ass momma?"

"My momma living her best life. She single, so she can live how she choose to," she said in her mom's defense..

"Well, how do you live, when you're out of town on your single shit?" I pressed.

"First of all, I don't be acting single. We been together for years and we don't have any official titles," she said with accuracy.

"What we need with titles? You belong to me," I confirmed.

"Yeah and you belong to everybody else. I'm tired of this shit," she complained.

"I don't belong to everybody else. Why all these complaints suddenly out of nowhere?"

"It isn't out of nowhere. You make me feel like I ain't shit, and all of this material stuff means the world to you," she argued.

"I'm proud of my accomplishments and the things I'm able to afford us," I insisted.

"You should be, but you didn't accomplish these things by yourself."

"Girl, you wasn't with me shootin' in the gym," I recited.

"I'm not laughing. Before, we would have stopped arguing and proceeded to make up just so things can go right back to the way they were. I've been reevaluating some things," she revealed.

"You actin' all moody. You ain't pregnant are you? Cause if you is, I know it ain't mines!" I responded.

"Naw, I ain't pregnant," Stormy said.

"That ain't the answer you normally give," I remembered.

"I'm not in a normal kind of mood. You always think you know everything. I heard that song,"Stormy Monda,"and it's depressing."

Maintaining my focus and not falling for the bait, I continued, "You usually would say that if you was pregnant I'm the only one who could be the father. So now the question is who you been fucking besides me?" I questioned seriously.

I paused and stared intently into her left eye, which always blinked when she was lying. That body reading skills I got from the riverboat gambler. Her left eye blinked and it was a mental picture I took like a camera.

"You been fuckin' somebody else? Answer me! We might as well head back to my house, cause' ain't no since in spoiling everybody else appetite since you want to be a hoe," I said feeling betrayed.

Her smart aleck rebuttal in the middle of my U-Turn, "I ain't never been a hoe!"

I smashed the brakes. My tires screeched nearly crashing my car on the curb, and I yelled, "Well promiscuous then."

"Whatever," Stormy said.

"You still ain't said nobody, so who the fuck is it?" I demanded. When I saw the pause and the head drop, I knew my accusations were true. Hurt, but I didn't show it. Poker face the whole way. "Who is it? That's the last time I'm asking you," I demanded angrily.

She responded, "Forever." That name would go down in infamy.

Chapter 18

"Forever, who? The rap nigga? You mean to tell me you fucking with a young nigga? You just preached to me that power is silent. You go and get you a nigga who wears everything he's worth around his neck," I pause taking a deep breath, trying everything not lose my composure. "So now you want me to grow locs like that rap nigga you fuckin', huh. I brought him to the REC to talk to the kids and he fucked my bitch?" I asked not expecting a response.

"I ain't gonna be too many bitches," she said sternly.

"Well quit actin like one then."

"What you think you act like? You bring people to tell kids one story while you're in back rooms making deals that possibly put drugs on the streets, or on the phone breaking one of them kids momma's hearts," Stormy accused.

"Now, I'm slanging drugs and breaking kid's momma's hearts? You're pitiful," I shook my head in disbelief.

"That's all you do is break hearts and dispose of people like trash. You are a coldhearted greedy muthafucka. You ain't even mad that I'm fuckin' somebody else. You're more upset about who it is," she spoke with disappointment in her voice.

"Why you want me to get so upset, cause' you're going through a midlife crisis. Just like your momma did your daddy," I dug deeper.

"FUCK YOU!" she yelled, adding salt to the wound.

"NO! FUCK YOU!" I screamed at the top of my lungs.

"I can't even get a good morning text from you. No how is your day going, or even a good night call, cause' you're most likely with someone else," Stormy reflected.

"Don't try to blame this shit on me," I told her as we walked. I didn't hold the door open to my place, but the air seemed more colder than usual.

"It's true. You treat me like I'm a random chick out here in these streets," she said. Her words fell on deaf ears while she burst into the half crack door to my sanctuary.

"You know how many times a woman has told me if she had someone else, she wouldn't be here with me? On more than one occasion, them same women have gotten calls from boyfriends or maybe husbands. They seemed to suck my dick better the more the phone rang. They opened up and let me fuck deeper as the text chimed. I refuse to be that nigga. I don't have to check up on you. You either where you say you at, or you ain't. You gonna do what you gone do, regardless. I ain't no babysitter," I explained. As I walked outside to the terrace, I heard all the traffic. She followed closely.

"But you babysit Church whenever his drunk ass is in town. The nigga didn't even have the decency to take the little price tag off the metts," she said.

"You fuckin' a nigga and you're talkin' about the price tag on the metts. Yo ass the one need a check," my words exposed the Heart Queen.

"You love your life in the most selfish and self-destructing ways possible. Church still dealing with women who house smell like roach spray and black and milds," Stormy fired back.

"What that got to do with you giving up the pussy," I asked, waiting on the answer.

She interrupted, "Hold on. Let me finish. You like being anchored to the very things that will sink your ship. If you still didn't feel guilty about him taking that case that he volunteered to do, you wouldn't keep repaying him over and over. He is a pawn with a crown."

"He's like a brother to me. We have been through all types of shit together. Shit you know nothing about," I corrected.

"I know enough. As much as you win, you must have some infatuation with losing. The degenerate gambler unable to walk away a winner," she said briefly pausing her verbal assault. She continued,"Power Riches Or Death, childish shit yawl into. Yawl need to grow up."

"How the fuck you telling me to grow up and you fucking a nigga 10 years younger than you? He sends you a good morning text with smiley face emojis and you reward him with some pussy?" I shouted, becoming more and more frustrated with every word.

"I fuck him, cause' he appreciates me. Makes me feel smart and it ain't just about the sex. You think this shit is a game that will never end… like we can always start over when you feel like it."

"That nigga name Forever, The Diamond King…."

Interrupting again Stormy said, "But he lives like tomorrow never comes and you live like tomorrow is promised. You go weeks without speaking to me as if I did something to make you mad. I can never please you.

I'm tired of your words cutting me and burning my soul instead of soothing me. You act like I ain't human. Hell, sometimes you act like you ain't human," she insisted.

"I don't want no love where respect ain't greater and no pussy that don't come with peace," I reminded her.

"That woman really did a number on you."

"What woman?" I asked.

Stormy refused to name names and she continued, "Whoever has you so cold and distant. You push everybody who loves you away and keep those who you love close, even if they mean you no good. Your lying ass uncle with the dirty ass fingernails…cheated you out of $10,000.00 and you still live and die by the things he told you like a boy hearing a fable for the first time."

"Yeah, he got me out of a few stacks, but that's on me. Other than that, he has always been there for me," I insisted.

"Been there for you? Ain't that the same uncle that didn't let yawl in when yawl didn't have nowhere to go in the middle of the night, and yawl slept in the hospital waiting room?" she asked already knowing the answer.

"It was tough love," I said in defense.

"Tough love? Yawl were children! Don't love me tough. I'm not the one you need to punish. I'm a good woman and I've been good to you," Stormy pleaded.

I ignored her pleas, "How you a good woman and you sucking another niggas dick? On that note, get your shit and get out! Leave the key on the…...." She flung that key with all of her might hitting me square in my heart. I looked down at the slightly bent key that she refused to quit jamming into the lock and ignored the pain as it pulsated and breathed. I couldn't let her see me flinch.

"The excitement is missing. Everything is predictable even your sex moves. We just fucked on a million dollars cash," Stormy said savagely.

Chapter 19

"Bitch, you better watch your mouth," I warned.

"Or what….,"she said with a bold, but false sense of confidence.

"I'mma throw you off this fucking ledge."

"You might, but then again you wouldn't lose all of this for me," she explained.

"Bitch you can't make me lose nothing. I will toss your ass over and meet the police when they are scraping you off the sidewalk in the front of the building. I got a million dollars plus in the safe in my office," I said moving towards her.

"You care about that money more than you do me," she screamed while backing up to the wall.

"And you're boasting about fucking a king to me. Bitch, I make kings for a living. I have more than his life is worth in my office and more than it takes to get rid of him in my pocket," I revealed.

I grabbed her neck lifting and bending her body over the ledge in my mind, I remembered three boys going into the woods and only two coming out. I choked her tighter. My hands like a noose on the Poplar tree. Her eyes bulged as blood vessels began to swell and pop while I swung her body from side to side. Her pretty green fingernails dug deep into my hands and arms, this time not for ecstasy, but to be free from the inevitable face of her death. The selfies she took with him during secret trips and shit all in her obituary. I was squeezing tighter as her fight began to leave and her arms seemingly lifeless dangled in the air like broken wings.

Suddenly, I saw a vision of me becoming this version of my father that I never wanted to be. I released my grasp. Her body crashed down like cupid with an arrow in his heart, leaving her to hang halfway off the edge. As she gasped for air, she slid down the wall like it spit between her ass cheeks.

Barely higher than a whisper, "You choke like a bitch!" came out of the mouth of the only woman whose love could weaken me once she was able to speak.

Incapable to stand, wounded and bowing like a defeated queen, she never lost strength to be defiant."Any of our businesses we have together I'm liquidating," I said wiping her foamy spit from my hand with a silk scarf that I got out of her purse. It was probably gifted to her from the boy king who took my kindness for weakness. "Dick will give you a fair settlement. I'm sure you'll have the paperwork this week," I said, throwing the soiled designer fabric to her feet.

As she gathered her luggage, the battered instigator made her way to the door bruised and teary eyed. "Just like that you're gonna throw everything away?" she said finally realizing the gravity of the situation.

"No, you threw everything away and just like that it's gone. If you wanted to scratch your itch there were plenty of niggas you could have fucked, but you violated by fucking somebody I brought into my home and has eaten at my table," I said angrily.

"King maker," she spoke with sarcasm and disgust."If there are too many kings wouldn't that be checkers and not chess?"

"Not if they aren't on the same board, it wouldn't be!" I said, slamming the door on that present truth. I stood at the closed door and remembered. In the past, I would have gone after her or she wouldn't have left. It would have been just silent treatment waiting to be canceled with the first good gesture our unspoken apology. Her copy of the key laid in the eye of the hurricane. As the bell from the elevator dinged, summoning

103

to take her away, the key was evidence of what once was, and proof of that lie.

Chapter 20

I hopped in the shower for real this time. I couldn't even look at the clock. Time will tell the tale that no man can ever tell, and I'm attentively listening. The water steamed, poured over my body, and burned as it cleansed the razor like marks and jagged scratches on my hands and arms. "Stormy Monday" played throughout the house chiming in as the blues man told our story like no one else could.

"Saturday, I go out to play," we sang in unison. Adrenaline still pumped, but it's nothing that a night out in the fresh air won't cure. Me and Stormy used to fuck so much in this shower when we weren't mad, or when we were making up. I can still see her face pressed up against the glass assuming the position and loving every minute of it.

The fact that she chose someone I practically helped get his break with my connections and exposure to different people, made the betrayal 10 times worse. I did make his mother cry on occasion, but that was because she wanted something that we clearly agreed wasn't the goal from the very beginning. Friends with benefits, nothing serious, and no feelings involved was the plan until she caught feelings, played on my phone and showed up uninvited. The situation was out of hand. I'm guilty for what I'm guilty for, but I refuse to be guilty for the things I didn't do. If it was revenge for his momma, then I guess he did what was necessary.

At the end of the day, I'm more pissed at Stormy, cause' she was supposed to isolate my weaknesses from the public and not help expose me by allowing herself to be available to anyone especially a king I made. Looking at the Diamond King's Instagram, he will be performing his new song "Nigga, I Fucked Yo Bitch" from his album "The Making of a Diamond King" at the new club in midtown tonight. This is where Stormy and her girls were headed tonight allegedly. I don't believe in coincidences. His momma violated rules and got her feelings hurt, and he violated rules that are going to hurt her feelings again. I'm a fair man, but this one isn't forgivable. You ate at my table and came into my house. I'm ending this game in two moves.

"Church, where you been?" I said through the phone. "I ain't heard from you all day. I texted and called you to let you know that situation got moved up to tonight. It sounded like you sent me to voicemail earlier. When you didn't text back, I knew you was laid up playing make up," he said like only he could.

"I don't have a missed call, or a text from you," I said slightly confused.

Damn, was that him I called when I was with Ice suspend in animation?

"Somethings wrong with that bootleg phone of yours, cuz I got that "CAN YOU HEAR ME NOW" top of the line phone," Church joked.

"Oh, nigga quit perpin'. You still fuckin with that Obama phone. HAHA," I laughed. "Did you handle that yet, or are you going to handle it now?" I inquired.

"This ain't one of those you can chip in and get a flip on. This is a straight swap. I know your greedy ass. You stay trying to get yours off," he accused.

"HAHA, shid you can't blame me," I said, shamelessly. My nigga do love them ratchets. But at the end of the day, I would rather have him by my side, cause' it ain't no fakery.

"Let me get back to you in a few. I will hit you up when I've handled this business," he said, disconnecting the call and wondering what the fuck kinda lick he finna hit.

Chapter 21

I walked out onto the terrace. It was my favorite place in the penthouse, because of the view, the fresh air, the memories, and even the arguments that turned into meaningful apologies that were a welcoming relief sometimes. This is my sanctuary where I have composed some of the very words that pay me while I sleep, and the same location where I have made deals that took that very sleep away.

For the first time in a long time, I'm paying attention to the other buildings, the thickness and the smell of the air that's not so fresh up here sometimes. The traffic was chaotic and gridlocked. The people were lost and fast moving. Stormy was right, I have greedily created too many kings and now those kings want to be the King maker. My chessboard had turned into checkers. Too many pawns wear crowns. There are imposters on thrones. I should have moved more wisely.

I naively assumed that the men I help build up would repay me with gratitude by helping others. That childlike mentality, for a king. It is a selfish position where you have subjects that are subjected to your rule, but are not equals. It's time to remove some more pieces off the board. Time to call in some loans and call in some favors. Their chaos will be my peace. Time for some of these straw houses to be brought down on themselves, and burned to ashes. Men I once thought of as family will be amongst the first sacrificed. Resenting me quietly, they will be removed kicking and screaming loudly against their will.

How could I possibly think that the boy king wouldn't harbor some resentment? I watched his mother cry over me. I was a mentor who chose to be the man I am, and not the man she wanted me to be. I was blinded by my own arrogance, and unable to see Stormy being whisked away by my enemies. I shared stories and he plotted against me. My weaknesses allowed me to be blindsided. It is time to evaluate and proceed. I was a king isolated in his castle. I wasn't in touch with the pulse
of the people, or the heartbeat of the hustle. I allowed money to be my only goal, as I built a castle made of sand. In the process, it was ready to crumble right beneath my feet. It is time to walk around a little bit, even if it's just briefly. I

became a king with a soldier's discipline, exchanged for a mercenary's greed.

Among the people walking, I observed the fact that most have no idea about the deals that are made above their heads. Deals that concerned their livelihood and wellbeing inside many of the buildings that towered just beneath the heavens. They were bold signs meant to symbolize their dominance while illuminating the night beyond the conspiracy theories and the rumors. The diseases and cure were created by the same people. The problem and the solution were utilized to divide the public. The mask of peace hid chaos in plain sight. The dope pushers were cops, judges, and lawyers. They protected friends in high places with policies they created to insulate them from recourse. Gangs were armed by the very people who were supposed to protect, serve, and defend our liberties. Their hopes of the complete annihilation of the lost natives fueled the fire of a master plan that had been in the making for centuries.

On a chessboard somewhere, I'm a pawn with a crown. In a league unknown to me, I wouldn't even get playing time. Amongst them, I am similar, and unaware of the realities that lie beneath the veil. I was in love with a dream of fast money and the thought of it lasting forever. Even though forever has yet to be seen and witnessed by anyone living.

Chapter 22

About 10 feet ahead of me was a man like the panhandler on the freeway exit. He had the same unkempt beard saturated with many years of smoking and poor hygiene, and he pushed a grocery cart. His nails were jagged and caked with a black substance, and his fingertips were brown like peach wood. Although we were going in opposite directions, we met at a point by his design. The wobbly front wheel on the grocery cart came to a sudden stop.

"Excuse me sir. Can you spare some change?" said the man whose breath smelled like hot garbage juice. His gum line was like mold in a basement. The rot grew from beneath his teeth. I looked hesitantly at this man with the matted hair, who smelled of piss and poverty. His camouflage jeans designed and stained with missed opportunities. His smile, genuine, but in his eyes, I saw the reflection of myself. I would be a king fallen, if I didn't execute my plan by any means necessary, regardless of the collateral damage. I gave the man whatever it was, as I reached in my pocket without looking.

I attempted to right my wrongs subconsciously in the presence of the universe's all-seeing eye.

While placing my hand in his hand, he took a hold of my hand and said, "I too am a king. I'm a king rising."

Puzzled, pausing briefly, I replied, "Well I hope this money can help you on your journey."

As I hurried along, my stomach turned and my head was spinning. No time to smell the roses, I thought.

"Thank you, sir. I appreciate it," he said.

Walking away, I headed further down the block to enjoy the sights.

He shouted, "What goes up must come down." These were the last words I heard from the prophet for profit as he continued his pilgrimage searching for disciples.

His wagon filled with cans and scrapped metal wobbled down the street. The fall isn't the scariest part. It's where I land that I'm defending against.

Chapter 23

My fortress was being destroyed from the inside like a cancerous parasite eating away at vital organs. Even though the prognosis seemed terminal, no long stint in hospice for me. I won't be looked down on by those that love me and hate me while the morphine drips until the plug is pulled and I flat line!

King maker no more. The throne abdicated. I would be replaced by a mask wearing traitor who once bowed before me promising loyalty. When I get back at the crib, I'mma take a nap before I get my night started. I didn't get what I wanted accomplished, just a sore dick and empty balls. Stormy had been on my mind ever since she left, and a piece of me left with her. What remained of me is married to this game, and the best thing I can be in a dream wedding is the best man. The big empty bed still smelled like earlier . Dried stains from the orgasms we shared. The I love yous that she traded for much less, than what she was getting from me. Out of all the dicks in the world, she chose that one and I can't get passed that. It might be viewed as hypocritical to some, but fuck'em. You should be who I need you to be, or be who you are with someone else. There is no compromise.

I hadn't heard from Ice. No text or anything. Is she trying to position herself for something different, or is she a piece that needs to be removed from the board. Turtle will be removed from the board. His sister Angie will be my intermission tonight. His player-hating ass has been doing too much lately. Although I celebrated with him, we should have been hoisting that trophy together, but he slyly cut me out. It probably was Martha's doing, gassing him up to do anything she told him. She keeps another man's dick in her mouth no matter how much he obeys her.

Chapter 24

Commotion outside of my door interrupted my dreamless sleep. I went to the door to see who it was half-dressed and disheveled. It was Detective Corral with a bunch of his uniformed buddies outside of my once peaceful palace in the sky. A piece of paper partially covered his smirk, while his shadow warriors anxiously awaited entry.

"What do I owe this pleasure officers?" I inquired.

"We have a search warrant to search your property," said the head of the lynch mob.

"Search my property for what?"

"It's all in the paperwork, Mr. Craft, but evidence regarding conspiracy charges for starters," he said.

"Conspiracy for what?"

"Some people seem to believe that this nice place you have was purchased with money you laundered through illegal enterprising. Tags and others you associate with are suspects and are wanted for questioning about some missing freight from the docks," he revealed.

"I need to call my lawyer. This is some bullshit!" I yelled as storm troopers watched silently.

"We're here doing our job. Please have a seat on a sofa and remain out of our way. If you didn't do anything you shouldn't have anything to worry about. Search the place fellas. Don't leave a stone or pillow unturned," he commanded.

Watching intensely as they searched, I tried to see by their movements if they were looking for something like my safe that's hidden away in my office. Only a few people know it exists, Stormy and Turtle. Turtle, because he installed it. I'm almost positive that I never showed Ice or Church. There isn't anything else here. I always keep my private life and business separate. The lead detective had wavy brown hair, clean shaved face, and a muscular build and made flamboyant hand movements. He sat down on the couch opposite of me trying to read my body language. The riverboat gamblers tutelage was on display again. Calm and collect, I didn't miss a beat or break a sweat.

"All questions, refer to my lawyer," I said emotionless. Yet, he continued badgering me, crossing his legs in the process, exposing his neon pink socks that screamed look at me as they clashed with the olive-green two-piece suit he was wearing. The brown leather loafers were hand made in Italy, and slightly scuffed at the bottom. I noticed it as he dangled his right foot.

"Laundry day?" I questioned pointing to his socks.

"No, asshole. These are for breast cancer awareness. My wife likes you, but I don't. I don't know what she sees in you, or that raunchy show that you put on," he said smugly.

This nigga perpin. We go to the same invitation only parties that will have the church lady clutching her pearls. My show pales in comparison.

"That's a nice Atlas statue you have there. You know, you guys are similar," he said.

"How so?" I asked pretending to be intrigued.

"Up here, you are condemned to hold up the sky just as he was. Mounting pressures from multiple direction forcing you to try harder for what used to be so easy for you," he expressed.

"I chose Atlas for his unwavering strength and ability to maintain his composure under pressure no matter what," I explained.

"Well Atlas, I guess we will see how much your strength wavers shortly."

"Nothing here boss, but sheets that smell of shit and fish, or just some shitty fish," his soldier shouted after seemingly taking forever, while sniffing my off-white sheet.

"You can have that sheet. Pussy is a dime a dozen. You know how many of those I can buy?" I said arrogantly.

The unnamed officer took another whiff of the sheet, wiped his crotch with it, and tossed it to the side like I have did towels so many times. If it was a strategy to somehow unravel me, it wasn't going to work.

"Here you go," the dirty detective smirked and tossed me a bullet the same caliber from the woods years ago.

It was made by the same manufacture that lay lodged in a skull that the riverboat gambler was supposed to get rid of for $10,000.00. The payment was cleverly disguised as a game of three card Monte. Stormy stood attentively watching. My theatrics were to protect her and control the narrative. Catching the bullet, prevented him from having any satisfaction of seeing me fumble under pressure.

"Someone will be in contact with you, Craft. As for that slick nigga Tags, the green light is lit for him and anyone who he associates with. That freight was covered with high-end heroine and pure fentanyl. They should have never let you niggas think yawl was kings," Detective Corral said.

The death squad exited with their guns unholstered as if to be waiting to kill me where I stood. The head dick and messenger spit on the mirror in the foyer, cause' he probably hated his own reflection. Here I am shaken, but stoned faced. I haven't drunk in years, but a shot would be life right now. They are trying to take it all and remove me off my chessboard in grand fashion. Atlas, with his wish granted. His curse removed before realizing that he preferred being condemned to hold up the sky.

Chapter 25

Dick didn't answer his phone which is not that unusual. If he doesn't call back in the next few minutes, then I know that the sky is falling and Atlantis is sinking. This small caliber brass bullet reminded me of much darker time seeing Church and the boy king go into the woods together. He was a monster, terrorizing the neighborhood, beating up girls and boys. Four years older than us, at least 2 feet taller, he was in and out of youth detention centers and foster homes all his life.

A hateful muthafucka that no one liked, but even some adults feared. Hands as big as baseball mittens. His skin dirty brown. The whites of his eyes, a mustard yellow. Every time he gave out pain, he would smile revealing the hole where his front tooth used to be. A three-inch scar on his face looked like a centipede. I rushed into my uncle's house to get his pistol from his nightstand under his old army jacket. I stuck the loaded deuce deuce in my front pants pocket along with the moncy I hustled up earlier, and headed to the woods to find my friend and the boy king.

"Church!" Church!" I repeated with no response stepping into the shallow creek heading towards our hide out. Salamanders and Tadpoles slithered and swam for safety as the water rippled.

"Church! Church!" my voice echoed through the trees. The birds panicked and flew away. Leaves, a variety of autumn hues, fell to the ground. Muddying my school shoes to find my friend, I knew that was an ass whoopin in the making, but I didn't care. Behind the old cardboard boxes that once housed T.V.'s, I found the boy king sitting on a milk crate with my friend's face in his lap. He was holding his head down with his dick in his mouth forcing Church to pleasure him. When he saw me he didn't flinch. He wasn't startled. The giant man-child had no fear.

He looked at me straight in the face, "You're next bitch!" he shouted.

I panicked. My first thought was to run, but I was too scared and my legs wouldn't move. I was frozen in time like a statue.

"You scared like a lil bitch. I'm fucking yo pretty eyes ass," he insisted.

I pulled out the gun. I was shaking and my mind was racing.

"Let him go NOW, NIGGA!" I screamed mustering up all of the strength in my manhood as possible.

He still refused like death was just a temporary moment. "You never pull a gun on a man and don't use it," said the voice of the halo eyed mentor. That lifelong advice echoed.

"Kill me! Take me out of my misery," he screamed.

In that moment, I pulled the trigger hitting the tree just an inch off from hitting him. The second shot hit the monster in the forehead before he had time to move, or I could change my mind. We both remained committed to our destinies. Death wasn't instant. He fell back in anguish causing the cardboard boxes to collapse on top of them. I went into the pile to uncover my friend from beneath the rubble. The monster's dick still exposed nearly severed by the teeth of his child victim. Shaking and bleeding from the mouth, he gagged on his own blood. Using the butt of the gun to finish him off, I gave a blow for every day he tortured us. For every day he took our stuff when we left the store, and most of all for molesting my friend.

Unable to move the large man child, we went frantically to get my uncle from the pool hall where he spent most of his time hustling pool or playing cards. Tall, slender, and dark as night, he walked with an authority I have seen only in a few men. A chemical explosion damaged his corneas and left his eyes with permanent halos in them. You can tell that he knew death personally, and dealing with it was just a walk in the park. After prying him from the pool hall, we took the grave digger to the scene to help us dig a grave for the monster, boy king. Our now deserted cardboard palace reduced to a pet cemetery. The berries were placed inconspicuously on the dirt pile like a tombstone for the monster's grave with no name. We found out later that the child predator was molesting several kids in the neighborhood. He tricked them with candy and money.

Chapter 26

I looked around at the house and everything was in disarray. I don't know what they were looking for. I don't know if this was just an elaborate way to deliver the message, or to unsettle me. I don't feel lonely, but I know that I'm alone. At this point, it's not necessarily a bad position to be in. I'm not sure who to trust, or who not to trust. The thought of having a drink passed. I refuse to be anything, but a king rising. What goes up must come down. That's just the nature of life. Right now, I need to see whose mirroring my moves, and striking me before I can strike with such precision. My team has been exposed. It was a kingdom, in principle, but no longer in domain. My safe, hidden behind a special corridor, was not easily accessible without prior knowledge, or specific instructions. "WHAT THE FUCK!!!" I said.

My safe empty! No cash and no bonds. Information about my offshore accounts, trust accounts, life insurance policies everything had been taken. All of my life work replaced revealing all of my life past. Speechless, closing my eyes in disgust, I slammed the safe door shut.

Hard for me to breathe, rage, and acid from my stomach raced to see who would be released first. The aged Cognac in the crystal decanter was eyeing me as if it was what was needed to help me stand again, or to finish me off. Barefoot and disheveled, the whites of my eyes were red and watery like the panhandler at the expressway exit. My reign was over. My rock bottom was here. My present truth, I definitively lived out loud.

"Fuck that shit. Get a hold of yourself!" I said trying to convince myself.

Chapter 27

A king dethroned and robbed without a gun, I was nearly bankrupt before I was able to defend myself in war. I foamed at the mouth reaching for the bottle of rare Cognac gifted by someone who I don't remember for an occasion I'm not concerned with. I removed the top from the bottle. Nothing but silence echoed, as the pressure released into the atmosphere. The smell aggravated my stomach, repulsed by this level of weakness, I lunged the bottle without taking a drink, and the Atlas statue came tumbling down. The bottle smashed against the wall. The statue landed on the floor beneath it.

"Shit!" I yelled.

I examined the broken art to see if it could be fixed. The inside revealed lenses and mirrors like a camera. A Trojan horse, a knight to put the king in check stood frozen, and my queen was gone to be with her little king. My phone was gone. I didn't know where it was, and Church was probably drunk and doing whatever. Dick hadn't called. I know he can't be that damn busy. Ice hadn't called. If she did, I didn't know, cause' the death squad probably stole my phone. Is it Isis trying to checkmate me? Was the statue just smoke and mirrors the whole time? I searched relentlessly for my phone; my lifeline in this landfill full of things that I own. The only possession that could help me now. Phone numbers and account information to verify my identity. My phone was under the pillow, between the couch cushion, along with the bent key that fell there when I went to sleep.

"Thank God!" I said relieved.

The phone rang and the number was unavailable. I hit ignore and proceeded to call my fat lying ass lawyer.

The unavailable number called back and this time, I answered.

"What the fuck do you want!" I commanded through the phone suffering from post-traumatic stress syndrome.

"Hold up chill. This Pace. Damn, brother what's wrong with you?"

"My homie from the REC. I've been trying to reach you for a few days. Why the fuck you calling me from a private number?" I questioned.

"Shit, I completely forgot I'm calling you from the job. For some reason, it just does that. I'm calling, cause' your check bounced. That check that you sent us last week bounced for the KING MAKER program," Pace said.

"Ain't no way. The fuck you mean it bounced? I have more than enough money to cover that. Those funds are allocated from a trustee through a private trust," I responded.

"I just know it bounced and I figured I should bring it to your attention before you accumulate fees and stuff like that. Ain't no big deal. I know you got it. I just figured it was an error. By the way you know The Diamond King's party is tonight. Are you going? I know yawl used to be real tight. You was practically his stepdaddy for a minute," he said.

"Let me get to the bottom of this check situation," I said hanging up the phone without responding.

Chapter 28

Dick finally returned my call and I asked, "Where have you been?"

"I got your message . That business wasn't official. That is a hit squad Detective Corral had been under investigation for a while now. He has some pretty serious people backing him, because he basically does what the fuck he wants," Dick stated.

"What the fuck was he checking here for? I don't have anything to do with that business on the docks. Who the fuck robbed me? My safe is empty. Everything is gone!" I said as panick overtook my calm.

"I'm not sure Craft. Do you want to file a police report? You hang with some pretty unsavory characters, so it could be a multitude of people," he accused.

"No, I can't. That paperwork was done by Tags. But I do need to change my security codes on my offshore accounts."

He texted me the information. I was able to secure the offshore accounts. The funds were good, but I needed to get in contact with Bishop Blessings and see how the trust account for the program was bouncing checks. That account was set up to make money nearly forever if things were done properly. Dick said something that is so right. What if this is a concerted effort and not just random attacks from people that are close with theatrics to control the narrative?

Chapter 29

The Diamond King was the least of my worries. I needed to find out who was trying to dig up a monster. I called my brother immediately. He had since moved back home to take care of my Uncle who now must have a portable oxygen machine due to severe emphysema from smoking, and cirrhosis of the liver from drinking.

"What's good," I said to the man who threw me a lifeline without asking for anything in return.

"Unc has been waiting on your call. He said your check bounced for his private nurse and hospice care. Plus, he hasn't received the money he used to get every month for his living expenses," my brother said.

"Yeah it was brought to my attention that it is something going on with several of my trust accounts. I'm trying to contact the trustee as we speak," I informed.

"I need to speak to Unc. Put him on the phone."

"He ain't been feeling well. That new medicine has been making him sicker and very weak." I could hear the rumblings in the background. "Hold on, he said he wanted to talk to you," my brother relayed.

"Hello," I said, waiting for the ailing king maker to respond."

"I am very disappointed in you," Unc said, followed by a deep breath and a cough. You have put the empire in shambles, because you wanted friendships instead of rulership. Giving crowns to pawns and having them believe they are kings is fine. Instead of the pawns that they really are, you would treat them like kings. The board is over saturated and they have mounted a defense against you. You didn't see it coming, because you're too busy fucking and playing internet personality instead of expanding your territory with power, wisdom, charisma, and the wealth that has been accumulated in various businesses," he breathed deeply.

Chapter 30

There was some machine in the background beeping. I interrupted, "Unc you good?" I could hear my brother in the background.

Unc ignored my brother's concern and continued, "I always told you that boy in the woods was a king. He was misguided, but he understood force was necessary even in the appearance of peace. You're tip toeing around like the kingdom isn't yours."

"I ain't tip toeing around," I said.

"Don't you fucking interrupt me!" he commanded. "Turtle was a fucking coward. He cut you out of the deal worth millions, and you went to his house and celebrated instead of burning it down with everyone inside. Kings don't have to be perfect, but they do have to defend their honor and respect. Your name alone should have a young boy too much in fear to approach your woman, let alone fuck her on your million dollars," he lectured.

"What the fuck! That was my money!" I exploded.

"She is a good queen, but her vindictiveness is her downfall. She does shit intentionally to hurt you, to get a response like a child seeking attention from their parents. She never was going to spend the money. She thought you would have recognized that it was gone and confronted her. When I held her hand, I could see the tortured soul in her eyes. She was a child who has been involved in the dark side of things for a while. Misled and molested by the very ones who was supposed to protect her. She will do anything for you, if you are the king she wants you to be. She needs to be removed from the board permanently. She doesn't want to rule under you. She wants to rule you, by ruling your heart, and twisting your mind. The magnitude of your incompetence is that a million plus dollars was stolen from your house out of your safe, and you didn't realize it until weeks later. What do you have to say for yourself?" he paused, demanding a response.

"I fucked up, Unc! Too busy trying to build my brands and expand my businesses," I admitted.

"That's is the responsibility of those you handed crowns to. Not so they could build up and feel more independent, but so they would be eternally indebted to you. That guilt would riddle their bones before they would ever disappoint you by saying no to your requests. No matter how outlandish, you don't make kings to build sandcastles with you. You make kings to have a vested interest in their empires. That part you have right. It's this equality shit that has gotten into your mind. A king has no equals, especially to the ones that you placed in the position to be kings. They are forever your servants, or they will be permanently removed. There is no compromise. There is no negotiations."

Chapter 31

Walking back and forth, I paced as Unc gave me the information from a thousand miles away on his deathbed. Information I should be giving him. He knows more about my business than I do. But how? Thinking to myself while walking onto the terrace, my left foot slightly numb, I noticed that it is a trail of blood behind me, because I stepped in some glass. I didn't even bother putting a bandage on it. I let the blood run. Self-mortification was a sacrifice to the universe. Somehow, I would be resurrected as a king rising. There was a tip of a fingernail that had to come off Stormy's hand. In disgust, I threw it off the ledge symbolic of her falling from heaven. Like a vacuum, the gravity pulled what was left of her to the pavement below.

"Quit fucking daydreaming," he said, as if he was looking directly at me. "You babysit Church out of guilt, but he knows his position is to be a pawn that is why he took the case for you. He did his job. You allowed strays to be strays, and pawns to be pawns. It is a necessary balance in life, war, and evolution. You have the makings to be a great king, but you are trying to put friendships that are fragile and temporary before the legacy that will feed our family for generations. You are the King Maker. They don't make you, you make them. Do you really believe Church and the boy king never been in that wooded area alone before? Were you too young to remember the rumors, or are you in denial?" Unc continued to advise me. "Think back."

Closing my eyes as if being hypnotized by the glowing halos of the master teacher, I heard him continue,"Was Church being forced to go, or was he going voluntarily"

"I can't remember. I just remember seeing them. I didn't want him to hurt my friend," I said sadly.

"You're not little boys anymore. Church is a liability. After he removes Tags from the chessboard, I want you to remove him," he replied.

Chapter 32

Damn, so that's what he's down here on. I looked out over the edge at nothing but darkness. There were no lights or cars. It looked as if I was down in a bottomless pit.

"Church's business is simply to remove the cancer. You fed Tags too much. He started to swell in the head and making side deals. Those cars were worth millions of dollars once processed. Somehow, he forged the paperwork to remove damn near a hundred cars. He is one of your biggest threats. Just so happen, I knew someone close to the situation, and I was able to insulate you. That shake up was to get your attention and remind you, that I am the one who controls the narrative. I have men fearing me still even as I lay here dying. I have taken lives and lives will be taken, because what is necessary isn't about right or wrong. That is for those sheep that go to buildings to worship God. When there is limitless sky, that represents God's abundance. It's time for you to get your hands dirty again. You have forgotten the smell of iron as the blood that pours out and oxidizes. Maybe, it's amnesia that made you forget how it felt for life to end by your hands.

"Do you remember the rabid raccoon that used to tear through the trash every night for us to clean up every morning?" he asked.

"Yeah I remember that. Do you remember how we stopped that oversized rodent from doing that? We sat a trap with some leftovers," I said.

"And then what?" Unc asked

"You told me to slit his throat," I answered.

"What did you do?" Unc questioned.

"I cut his head off?" I confessed.

Unc asked, "Why did you do that?"

"Because it is better to overkill than under kill," I said bluntly.

"That's the kind of king that rules forever. Even after, he is gone from the physical, his name and reputation besieges people with respect, and then fear. Some will even claim to be devoted and love him, but it's the repercussion that keep them in check. Move forward king and remove the pieces from your board and reclaim your kingdom," he encouraged.

As if the trance was over, my sight returned. I was able to hear and see all the land before me that I will acquire for my family for generations to come.

www.ingramcontent.com/pod-product-compliance
Lightning Source LLC
Chambersburg PA
CBHW060423260626
47161CB00005B/1764